Ash pulled a lollipop out of the pocket of his coat.

Levi looked at him with suspicion, but took it and stopped crying.

"Where were you when I was trying to dress him?" Jordan rolled her eyes at Ash and he couldn't help but laugh.

"Next time I'll do better."

She clicked the car seat harness into place and closed the door.

He shoved his hands into the front pockets of his jeans. "I'll come by and check on him tomorrow. And you can call me if you need anything."

She nodded and her eyes lingered on his for a long second. "I'm sure we'll be fine."

Jordan rounded the car and got in, turning around to give her little charge a reassuring smile. Ash watched as she drove out of the parking lot.

Yeah, she was different. Not his type at all. So why was he so interested?

Award-winning author **Stephanie Dees** lives in small-town Alabama with her pastor husband and two youngest children. A Southern girl through and through, she loves sweet tea, SEC football, corn on the cob and air-conditioning. For further information, please visit her website at stephaniedees.com.

Books by Stephanie Dees

Love Inspired

Family Blessings

A Baby
for the Doctor

Stephanie Dees

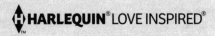

LOVE INSPIRED BOOKS

Recycling programs
for this product may
not exist in your area.

ISBN-13: 978-0-373-62307-5

A Baby for the Doctor

www.Harlequin.com

Printed in U.S.A.

Many are the plans in a person's heart,
but it's the Lord's purpose that prevails.
—*Proverbs* 19:21

Man plans, God laughs.
—Old Yiddish Proverb

For my favorite three-year-old—
you've had my heart from the moment I saw you.

Special thanks to Melissa Endlich and the
editorial team at Love Inspired and to
Melissa Jeglinski and the Knight Agency.
I'm so thankful to be able to work with you!

Chapter One

Jordan Conley's phone rang for the third time in as many minutes. She gave her horse Bartlet one last scratch on the neck and nudged him out of the way. "Sorry, old boy. Three calls in a row is a distress signal."

She tossed the curry comb into the pail next to the stall and dug her phone out of her back pocket. It was her twin sister. "Claire?"

"Oh, thank God you answered."

Jordan could hear the newest baby, the one they called Sweetness, screaming in the background. "What's up?"

"Sweetness has a double ear infection. And the principal at Kiera's school called. She punched a girl in last period and they won't put her on the bus. I have to pick her up right now."

"What do you want me to do?"

Claire sighed. "I just got a call from the county. They need someone to pick up a three-year-old boy at the hospital. I told them twice we couldn't do it. They just called again and said they're going to have to keep him at the office tonight if we can't take him."

"Where do I pick him up?" Already Jordan's mind was sifting through what she needed to do to make it happen. She didn't have time for this. Of course she didn't. She could barely manage the horses' upkeep much less build her therapy practice, but there was a three-year-old in a hospital with no one.

She had a therapy session at five she could postpone. Opening the door to the tack room, she grabbed a toddler car seat from the storage closet, hauling it out the door of the barn before heading into the big house, where Claire and Joe lived with their—at least for the moment—eight kids.

A shuffling pause and Claire was back. "Sorry. He's in Mobile in the Children's Unit. The resource manager said he was hurt pretty bad but didn't give me any details. No, Georgia, no Cheerios in your ears. Anyway, I don't know what you're going to find when you get there."

Jordan rummaged through a stack of children's pajamas and pulled out trains in a size 3T and rocket ships in 2T. She shoved them in a spare diaper bag and grabbed a couple of diapers out of a basket labeled *fives*. "So basically, it's situation normal."

"Basically. Okay, I just pulled in at the school. I've gotta go. Thanks, Jordan."

Even before her sister hung up the phone, Jordan was zipping up the diaper bag. She grabbed an apple on the way out the back door and tossed the diaper bag into the front seat of her old truck. The car seat, with its many hooks and straps, went into the back seat.

She'd learned a lot of new skills since she and Claire started fostering. Things like the temperature a bottle needed to be and that all diapers weren't created equal.

That little boys didn't really care how shoes looked, only that they were "fast."

She'd learned that she'd never met a night terror she didn't hate. And kids who had been through what their kids had been through were rightly scared of the dark. She learned that parenting, especially foster parenting, was exhausting, exhilarating and humbling.

When Claire and Joe got married and Joe and his daughter moved into the big renovated plantation house, Jordan had moved to Joe's cabin on the other side of Red Hill Farm, which she and Claire had inherited from their biological father. This setup actually worked better for her, since she was working to build her equine therapy practice, Horses, Hope and Healing. But still, with eight kids, there was always a baby to feed, homework to help with, hair to be fixed.

Her phone buzzed again. A text from Claire.

Forgot to tell you the caseworker is meeting you at the hospital with the paperwork. Baby's name is Levi Wheeler.

Yes, a name was kind of important.

Ash is on his way, too. We were in his office when we got the call.

Her heart stopped beating for an almost imperceptible second. Ash was the town pediatrician and her brother-in-law. And he was the most perfect human being she had ever met. She wasn't even sure she liked him because when it came to Ash, she turned into a klutzy teenager every time she got close to him. As if going through that stage once wasn't enough.

She pulled out of the driveway onto the highway and began to pray, one of those new skills she'd acquired. The children who came to live at Red Hill Farm brought heartbreak and grief and trauma. Since she couldn't take it away from them, the only alternative was to walk through it with them, and to do that, she needed Jesus. That had become abundantly clear very quickly.

Surround that little boy with Your peace, Lord. Heal his wounds, body and spirit. Let him never feel ashamed for what others did to him. Let him never feel unloved, unwanted, unworthy. He is Your child, Lord. Yours. Give me the strength and courage to be Your body, Your welcoming arms, for this child.

There were other things that were hard, but the prayers came easy.

At the hospital she walked through the doors, looking for the information desk, and ran into Ash. Her bags went flying, arms flailing.

When he put his arms out to steady her, her heart started thumping in her chest. He had on a pale blue pinpoint oxford cloth shirt and a crisp white lab coat with his name embroidered on the pocket. *Ashley Sheehan, MD*.

"You okay?" His summer-sky eyes were concerned.

"Fine, thanks." She realized she had the lapels of his formerly pristine lab coat fisted in her hands and loosened her grip with a wince. "Sorry."

Jordan took a step away from him and brushed off her jeans, noticing a brown smudge that she really hoped was just dirt. No wonder Ash didn't see her as dating material. The supermodel types he went out with wouldn't be caught dead wearing horse poop. Laughing at herself now, she leaned down to collect her stuff. "Have you seen our little patient yet?"

"Not yet. I was waiting for you. He's in room 314."

The caseworker, Reesa, a petite woman with a riot of lavender curls, was waiting for them as they got off the elevator on the third floor. "Hey, guys, they're about to discharge Levi. He's been treated for chemical burns, tape burns, neglect. Cops called us when they picked up the parents for cooking meth."

Jordan's eyes stung. She wouldn't cry. Not in front of the caseworker—not in front of Ash—but already she wanted to weep. "He's three? Any family?"

Reesa started down the hall. "Not that anyone is willing to tell us about, so there won't be any visits, at least for now. I'll let you know if that changes. And yes, he's three, but he's small. He's also scared of me, so I'm going to let you two go in. The nurses said you can dress him and get him ready to go."

She stopped in front of a door. "Jordan, here's your paperwork. He's officially being placed with you and you will sign the discharge papers."

Jordan nodded. "And Claire?"

"Let's talk about that sometime next week." Reesa handed her the folder and backed toward the elevator. "For now your name is on the placement letter."

The weight of what she'd agreed to sat heavily on her shoulders. Not knowing what to expect was always hard for her. She liked life on her own terms, and being a foster parent was pretty much the opposite of that.

As Reesa disappeared down the hall, Jordan shoved

the papers into the pocket of the diaper bag and looked at Ash. "You ready?"

When he nodded, she pushed the door open. Room 314 was silent, shadowy. The only light on was the one over the bed, which highlighted the tiny boy. He might be three but he wasn't even the size of the average two-year-old. Curled up in sleep, he looked more like an infant.

She stopped halfway to the bed. He had bandages around his wrists and ankles, and gauze wrapped around his midsection. Dressed only in a diaper and covered partially by a sheet, he was unmoving in the bed.

Ash touched her arm. "Do you want me to go first?"

She shook her head. Levi was so still and quiet that she thought he was asleep, but when she rounded the end of the bed, she realized that his eyes were open and fixed on the window. "Hey, buddy."

Levi startled, but he didn't look at her. She reached into the bag she'd so haphazardly packed and pulled out a lovey, as Claire's kids called them. She placed it near his fingers.

Next out of the bag was the smaller pair of pajamas, which she realized would still swallow him. But actually, that might be better over the bandages.

"How about I take a quick look before you dress him?"

At the sound of Ash's deep voice, Levi started to shake, and he curled into a protective position, knees at his chin.

Jordan longed to pick him up and bring him safely into her arms, but she knew that he wouldn't feel safe there—not yet. Looking over at Ash and meeting his eyes, she gave him an apologetic shrug. "Maybe if you give us a few minutes."

Ash nodded and backed toward the door. "I saw Dr. Lowenstein at the nurses' station. I'm going to get his thoughts on Levi's care from here on out and take a look at the chart before he's discharged."

She studied the baby in the bed. Levi was in near fetal position, his thumb in his mouth, dark brown eyes wide and terrified. She'd gentled a lot of fearful horses in her time, horses who had been mistreated and neglected. Maybe teaching this little boy that she could be trusted wasn't so different.

Jordan pulled the rocking chair close to the bed, close enough to touch him. The first thing she did with a skittish horse was get them used to the sound of her voice. She began to sing to Levi, a little song she'd learned as a child. He glanced at her and looked away, but he didn't cry.

She heard the door softly latch as Ash closed it behind him. If she could just act like a normal human being around the handsome doctor, they could be friends. Instead, she was as awkward as a seventh grader at her first boy-girl party.

But there was no slow dancing here in room 314. Nothing to worry about. She smiled into a toddler's troubled brown eyes. Levi was the new man in her life now.

Ash leaned against the wall outside the door of the hospital room where Levi Wheeler rested. Nausea churned in his stomach—not at the wounds; he'd seen worse. No, he had to make an excuse to get out of the room because the thought that the very people who were supposed to love and protect this little boy were the ones—

Our God is a great big God and He holds us in His hand...

Jordan's sweet voice carried through the closed door. He didn't know how she could sing about God right now. Where was God when that baby's parents duct-taped him into a chair and left him there for days?

Ash's hand curled into a fist but he resisted the urge to punch the wall, instead choosing to walk the few feet to the nurses' station. "Levi Wheeler?"

The nurse selected the chart and handed it across the counter. "I haven't seen you in a while, Dr. Shee-han. You have time for a coffee? I've got a break coming up."

Flashing the smile was automatic. "I don't today. Rain check?"

He looked over the notes that Dr. Lowenstein had left in Levi's chart and glanced back at the nurse. "You have his discharge papers ready?"

"Yes, sir." The pretty blonde looked up at him from under her lashes.

He sighed and then forced the appropriate words. "Thanks, Amber. Let's see if we can get this young man out of the hospital."

She squeezed his arm as she walked by him. He stabbed his fingers through his hair, annoyed in spite of himself. His siblings were always making fun of him for his dimples, blond hair and blue eyes. And sure, in high school and college, he'd loved the attention from the ladies. Now it was just a distraction.

He didn't want someone who liked him for his looks. He wanted to spend time with someone who was interested in what he thought, what he cared about. He would never tell his brother, Joe, this, but he wanted a soul mate, like Joe had found in Claire.

He sighed. Maybe it was best that he hadn't found that. Marriage and family might work for Joe, but it wasn't in the cards for him. He pushed open the door to little Levi's room.

Jordan had Levi dressed in navy blue fleece pajamas with rockets and moons on them. The toddler's big brown eyes, his eyelashes wet from tears, met Ash's for one long moment before he stared out the window again.

"He let you dress him. I didn't hear any screams."

She shook her head. "He wasn't happy about it, but he did let me touch him. Baby steps, I guess."

As Nurse Amber went through the discharge papers with Jordan, Ash made sure to stay close to the door, away from where his presence might upset Levi. Other than the terrified reaction when Ash had gotten close to the bed, the little boy had shown no interest in anything and had made no sound at all. The hospital had done some preliminary evaluations, but no one could tell at this point how extensive the damage to Levi might be.

Amber handed Jordan a stack of prescriptions and then said, "Okay, sign here and you're good to go."

When the orderly rolled the wheelchair into the room, Levi looked toward it, brown eyes going wide. As the orderly brought it closer, Levi began to whimper. And when Amber reached for him to put him in it, the little boy lost it.

He screamed and scratched, jerking away from the nurse until she gave in and dropped him back onto the mattress, where he collapsed, sobbing.

Jordan stepped toward the baby, putting herself between him and the wheelchair. "Please take that out of here. Now."

The orderly left without a word.

Jordan nailed Amber with a look. "I know it's against hospital policy but I'm going to carry him out. The chair is obviously terrifying to him and I can't let him be more traumatized."

She held her arms out to Levi, whose huge waif eyes were full of dark fear. "Come on, buddy, let's get out of here. No chair. Just you and me."

He didn't move. Ash was pretty certain that she was going to have to carry him out kicking and screaming, but suddenly, the injured toddler threw himself into her arms.

She paid exactly zero attention to the snot running down his face, just cuddled him close and grabbed the backpack she had brought with her.

Amber was between Jordan and the door. She held Jordan's gaze for another moment before she relented and stepped out of the way. "I'll make a note in the chart that Dr. Sheehan walked you out."

"Perfect. Ash, let's get this little guy out of here."

Pulling the door open, Ash stepped out of the way and Jordan walked past him without looking back. Levi's little arms were clenched around her neck, his face buried in the hollow of her shoulder.

Ash thanked the nurse and followed Jordan into the hall. He'd dated a lot of Ambers, girls who were pretty and sweet, smart even. Jordan was different. She didn't care about her hair. She didn't wear makeup, that he could tell. More often than not, she had something questionable staining her jeans and hay sticking in her hair.

But she had just stood up for Levi, knowing instinctively what he needed. In her therapy practice, he had seen her create magic between a child and a horse. She was complicated and gifted and stunningly beautiful, despite the fact that she obviously didn't notice.

Or maybe because of it. And every time he tried to talk to her, the words stuck in his throat.

In the parking lot, Jordan's truck beeped as it unlocked, and she tucked Levi into his car seat, gently brushing a curl off his forehead. Crocodile tears started down his thin cheeks. Ash pulled a lollipop out of the pocket of his coat and held it out to Levi. He looked at Ash with suspicion, but took it and stopped crying.

"Now you find a lollipop? Where were you when I was trying to dress him?" She rolled her eyes at Ash and he laughed.

"Next time I'll do better."

"Okay, buddy, here we go." Jordan clicked the harness into place and closed the door. In an unguarded moment, Ash saw grief and pain flash across her face before she shuttered it. "He's really hurt. I wasn't prepared for how badly."

He shoved his hands into the front pockets of his jeans. "I'll come by and check on him after clinic tomorrow morning. And you can call me if you need anything."

She nodded and her eyes lingered on his for a long second. "I'm sure we'll be fine."

Jordan rounded the car and got in, turning around to give her little charge a reassuring smile. Ash watched as she drove out of the parking lot, lifting a hand as she turned the corner onto the highway.

Yeah, she was different. Not his type at all. So why was he so interested?

Chapter Two

Jordan turned on the coffeemaker in the kitchen, but not before she added another scoop of ground coffee to the filter. While it was brewing, she laid her head against the cool stainless-steel surface of the refrigerator. She was exhausted.

Levi had shunned the crib altogether, opting to fight it out in the living room. He'd stayed awake until he absolutely could not hold his eyes open anymore, finally falling asleep staring into the fire she'd built in the big stone fireplace. His dimpled fingers were entwined in the fur of her German shepherd, who was glued to his side. She didn't know exactly what had happened to this baby but he was stuck in fight-or-flight mode.

It was heartbreaking. He needed to learn to trust that she would take care of him, but his body wouldn't let him. Even her dog, Gus, understood Levi had broken places and all they could do to fix him was just be there.

A soft tap at the door had her glancing up in panic, but Gus just lifted his head and woofed softly before laying it back down. She put her finger over her lips and let her sister, Claire, in through the French doors that looked out over the pond to the barn on the other side.

"Hey, I just came to see how our new little guy is doing. I brought you some clothes for him." Her sister's long brown hair was in a messy bun on top of her head, an oversize sweatshirt hiding her still tiny baby bump.

"He's asleep on the couch. The crib was a no-go."

Claire peeked over the back of the blue velvet couch. "Oh, sweet baby. Has he eaten yet?"

"No. I tried everything I had that was kid-friendly. He wouldn't even eat one of those applesauce pouches. I'm not really sure what to do."

Claire shook her head. "Maybe Ash will have some ideas. He's so tiny. It's hard to believe he's three."

"That's what the paperwork says, but it wouldn't be the first time the age was wrong on the paperwork." She poured coffee into a ceramic mug and topped it with cream so she could drink it faster.

"Amelia said she would take care of the horses this weekend so you can get Levi settled."

"Bless her." Claire's stepdaughter, Amelia, had bonded with the horses from the first time she saw them. If she was looking after the animals, Jordan could stop worrying about them. "How's Sweetness feeling this morning?"

"Cranky. I left her with Mrs. Matthews, eating breakfast. She loves those tiny pancakes Mrs. M. makes."

"Hiring her was the best decision ever." Jordan gave her sister a sideways glance. Claire had nearly burned the house down twice and all of them had eaten more than their share of NoodleO's. "Not that you weren't a good cook."

"I wasn't." Claire poured herself half a cup of coffee. "But Mrs. Matthews is and she needed something big to do after her husband, Vince, passed last year."

A whimper came from the couch. Jordan leaned over the back and pulled the soft fleece blanket over his narrow shoulders. Levi squinched his eyes shut and burrowed farther into the cushions.

"What did Ash say about him?"

Jordan topped off her coffee and stirred it. "Ash didn't really get a chance to check him out last night. Levi seems to have an objection to superhot male doctors."

Claire snorted her coffee. "I bet Mama J doesn't have an objection."

Jordan scowled at the nickname—and the observation. "Mama J thinks Dr. Sheehan should stick to his high-society girls."

"I think maybe there's more to Ash than meets the eye."

"If you say so." Jordan wasn't trying to be rude, but Ash was tagged in social media with a different girl every week, most of the time dressed in evening wear, attending some function or another. His day-to-day couldn't be further removed from her simple life here on the farm. She walked, mug in hand, to the window.

"Jordan…"

When she turned around, Claire's eyes were filled with tears. "I know I asked you to pick Levi up. I even thought he and Sweetness could maybe share a room. But my margin is razor-thin right now and now I know… he needs more care than I can give him."

Jordan's heart hammered in her chest. She'd kind of had a feeling this would happen. Somewhere in the back of her mind, where she tucked things she didn't want to think about, she'd had an inkling that when she said yes to Levi, she wasn't just saying yes for the weekend.

That didn't mean the idea of keeping him didn't scare her down to her toenails.

Claire met her at the window. "I know you work so hard with the horses and taking care of your practice. You have so much on your plate. I talked to Reesa and she said they would try to find another family next week."

"No." The vehemence with which she replied surprised even Jordan. She gentled her tone. "No. I said yes to Levi. Not you. I didn't know what I was stepping into, but we never do."

Claire nodded, her eyes still brimming. "No, we never do. It's worth it."

"If Mom hadn't thought so, we wouldn't be where we are now." A wry smile curved Jordan's lips. "So remind me of that in a week when I'd sell my left kidney for a night of sleep."

"I will, but you have some time to think about it and make sure that's what you want to do. Now I need to get back before Mrs. Matthews realizes she traded her retirement for indentured labor." Claire grabbed Jordan around the neck and squeezed, tight. "I love you. I hope you don't regret moving here."

"Never. I like a challenge."

Claire laughed and handed her the empty mug. "I'll be back for more later."

Jordan watched her sister swing off the porch onto the well-worn path to the main house. Claire was in her element at Red Hill Farm. She may be struggling a little being a mom while dealing with first trimester sickness, but their brood of kids was thriving here.

As Jordan walked the few steps into the living area, she realized Levi wasn't asleep anymore. His dark brown eyes were wide-open and staring at her. His thumb was in his mouth, the pale blue lovey she'd brought to the hospital clenched in his fist, his other hand in Gus's black fur.

He blinked, his lashes taking a long, slow dip.

"Hey, buddy, you hungry? Want something to eat?" Even though she knew he probably wouldn't know it, she made the sign for *eat* tips of fingers to mouth. Gus's tail thumped. "Not you, you dorky dog."

Levi didn't move, just looked at her. At least he didn't seem scared. "How about some milk?"

Again, she made the sign along with the word. He didn't respond. She'd tried a sippy cup last night and he'd refused it. It was possible, considering the neglect, that he'd only had a bottle. Luckily, she had one left from an overnight with one of their former foster babies. She poured milk into the bottle and, after a little thought, added a packet of formula because Levi could definitely use the calories.

Warming it just enough for the powder to mix, she shook it and showed it to him. His eyes brightened for the first time. She eased onto the sofa and sat beside him. He reached for the bottle, but instead of just handing it to him, she picked him up and put him on her lap, letting him rest against her chest.

He stiffened, but didn't pull away from her like he had last night. She put the bottle in his mouth and he wrapped his fingers around hers and took a few sips.

He pulled it back, looking at it like he wasn't sure what he was tasting.

"It's okay, buddy. Good stuff." She let him slide into the crook of her arm so that she could see his face. His eyes were open and, as he drank, he reached with one small hand to explore the hair that had fallen out of her ponytail to frame her face. The touch was so light, she barely felt it.

His hand dropped to his side and she felt him give a big sigh. Eyes drifting closed, he relaxed against her.

The privilege of being the person who got to hold this baby and offer him safety was not lost on her. He was beautiful, those long, dark lashes an inky smudge on his cheek. As the bottle slid out of his mouth, a milky peace settled on his face.

What a strange feeling it was to have someone else's child in her arms, completely dependent on her. She didn't want to risk him waking up, so slowly she moved one leg and then the other onto the couch and laid her head back, letting the sleepless night catch up with her.

Ash knocked on the door of Jordan's cottage. The place had been falling down when his brother, Joe, moved in, but he'd repaired it. Now with Jordan's touch, there were dark purple and gold pansies spilling out of pots on the whitewashed front steps. The front door was painted a bright coral and the ceiling of the porch a contrasting pale blue.

He would never have imagined that the colors would work but they did, and the eclectic place seemed to suit Jordan. He tapped lightly on the door. No answer. Glancing at his watch, he confirmed that it was nearly noon.

Maybe she was at the barn?

He knocked again, a little more loudly, and heard shuffling on the other side of the door. A few seconds later the door flew inward.

Jordan, the baby on her hip, squinted into the noon-day sunlight. She rubbed the heel of her hand in one eye. "Wow. Bright."

"I'm so sorry I woke you up. I brought food?"

"I could kiss you." She grabbed his wrist and pulled him in the door. Two bright pink spots of color appeared in her pale cheeks. "But I won't. I mean, obviously I won't."

He laughed. "You might want to reconsider when you see what's in the bag. I brought cinnamon bread from my sister Jules's bakery. Mom sent you sandwiches from the Hilltop for lunch and my sister Wynn is in town and made you a chicken casserole for dinner."

"You guys." She pushed the door open wider to let Gus out and Ash in. "Come on in. I assume you knocked more than once? I'm sorry. We were up most of the night."

"How's he doing today?" Ash laid the armload of supplies onto the kitchen island and began to unpack them into the refrigerator.

"He took a bottle, which I know he's technically too old for, but it just felt right. He's been asleep ever since."

Ash held up a brown paper bag. "Toddler formula. I think your instincts are on target. Even if he's three, he's probably developmentally delayed. Trauma and neglect have serious consequences. And... I'm not telling you anything you don't know already."

"He didn't sleep until around four, I guess. He doesn't

seem as scared as he was when I first got him home, but he doesn't cry so it's hard to tell." She brushed a hand over the dark curls. Levi flinched.

Ash shook his head. "Poor kiddo. He's had such a rough time."

Dark brown eyes opened and scowled at Ash. Jordan was right, though. He didn't seem terrified like he had in the hospital.

"You may not know it now, Levi, but we're going to be friends, you and I." Ash pulled a construction vehicle sticker out of his pocket.

Levi curled into Jordan's side, but his eyes were on the sticker.

Jordan idly ran a hand over the baby's arm, gentling him. He wondered if she did it on purpose or if it was just instinct to her, like the bottle. The morning sun poured in through the windows, touching her red hair with fire. She really was something.

"Have you taken him outside? We could take him on a walk, get him out of the house for some fresh air."

"Good idea. Let me throw some jeans and boots on. Don't want to be walking around the barn in…" Her voice drifted off as she noted his leather loafers.

He laughed. "A little horse manure won't kill me. I'll take him while you change."

Jordan shifted Levi to hand him to Ash, but the toddler was having none of it, and his arms locked around her neck in a vise grip. She sighed. "I'll sit him on the couch. Don't let him fall off."

"Yes, ma'am." As Jordan disappeared into the bedroom, Ash studied Levi. With his thumb in his mouth and big, dark eyes trained on Ash, he wasn't letting anything get past him. "I thought we made progress. Remember the lollipop last night?"

No response. They were going to have to do some testing on this little guy to see where his deficits were. Ash wasn't even sure that Levi could hear.

Jordan opened the door of her bedroom, her hair twisted into braids, a ball cap on her head and black Hunter boots over her jeans.

Levi's eyes followed her as she moved around the room. She smiled at him, her eyes shining. "Little man, you ready to go for a walk outside?"

When the toddler looked at the door as Jordan picked him up, Ash figured that answered his question about hearing. He could at least hear and understand some things. "Have you seen him crawl or walk?"

"No. I put him down on the floor a few times with a toy during the night but he didn't play. No crawling or walking. He sat in one spot and sucked his thumb, watching every move I made." She opened the door and stepped out onto the porch. "Wow, it's really nice out here this afternoon."

He grinned. "Spring in Alabama. Severe weather, freezing cold, warm, hot. It changes by the hour."

They walked along side by side. The farm was peaceful, in its way. *Pastoral*, he guessed, was the right word for it. The pond was pretty—clear and spring-fed. Chickens wandered the yard. Goats, horses and a couple of spoiled donkeys grazed in the pasture. Because it was Saturday, though, half a dozen kids, who looked like they might have multiplied, raced around the yard.

Ash loved kids. Kids were awesome. It was one reason he had chosen to work with them when it came time to select a specialty. He did not, however, want kids of his own. He was going to leave that up to Joe, because his brother now had enough kids for the entire family, certainly enough to assuage his mother's desire for grandchildren.

Gus, Jordan's dog, loped up, circling them, nosing Levi's jammie-clad foot. Jordan uttered a low "Heel" and Gus dropped into place by her side.

She stopped at the fence to the pasture. Claire's horse Freckles was closest and the most curious. He lifted his head and snorted. She laughed. "He wants his apple, Levi. What do you think we should do?"

The little boy bounced once in her arms, the most animated Ash had seen him. He popped his thumb out of his mouth and pointed at Freckles. Jordan dug a piece of an apple out of her pocket and held it out to Freckles, whose soft lips plucked it gently from the palm of her hand.

A cat twined through Ash's legs and around Jordan's.

"Mama Kitty," Jordan said to Levi. He pointed at the children climbing on a play gym that Ash had helped Joe build. "Kids." Levi nodded and stuck his thumb back in his mouth. Jordan watched the kids, who were screaming in laughter. "You know my sister and I were in foster care for a while. We were relinquished by our biological parents and placed with a family for adoption, but it didn't work out."

"I didn't know that."

"I had a heart defect when I was born and had to have heart surgery before I was a year old. I don't think the adoptive parents were prepared for a sick baby. They wanted to keep Claire, but the adoption agency refused to split us up. We were placed in a foster home."

"How long before you were adopted?"

"Our foster mom adopted us when we were about eighteen months old. I'm not sure why it took so long, but that's the system for you. Not everyone can have an idyllic childhood with Bertie and Frank as their parents."

"Yeah, not so much." As soon as the words were out in space, he regretted them. He didn't like to talk about his childhood, at least what he remembered of it. Too many years had been spent in a drug-induced haze after surgeries, chemo and radiation. "When kids are sick, it puts a real strain on the family."

Jordan silently fed another piece of apple to Freckles. When she finished, she looked at him, a quizzical expression in her ocean-blue eyes. "Are you speaking as a doctor?"

It was the perfect out. He could say yes and she would never question it, but what good would that do? "I had cancer when I was a kid. I spent most of two years in the hospital and then I was in and out all through school."

"That must have been so hard."

Her hand on his arm surprised him. He smiled, slid his fingers through his hair and looked away, embarrassed. "It was. No one in the family really talks about it much. Even me. Especially me, I guess."

"We don't have to talk about it, Ash." Her voice was gentle, but he knew she meant it. Being with her was easy, and maybe that was why he found himself wanting to stay. To watch the sun travel the afternoon sky, talk to Jordan, watch the little guy's eyes lose some of the wariness.

And that scared the mess out of him. Ash reached into his pocket for his keys. "I'm glad I got to see our little patient. Keep the cream on those irritated areas and stick with the formula for a while. I'll see you in a few days at the office for his formal evaluation."

Surprise hid in her eyes, but she nodded. "Sounds good. Thanks for the supplies."

His car was just on the other side of the yard in the driveway. Was he running away?

Yes, probably.

And he didn't have to dig deep into his psyche to figure out why.

Chapter Three

Jordan bargained with Joe and Claire's thirteen-year-old daughter, Amelia, to listen for Levi so she could do the morning chores with the animals. It cost her a drive into town to the middle school, but with Amelia safely at school, she and Levi had time for breakfast at the Hilltop before their appointment at the WIC—Women, Infant, Children nutrition—office.

The café was owned by Joe and Ash's mom, Bertie, and her blueberry pancakes were the best in the state. Jordan pushed the door open, the bell on the door jingling.

Bertie looked up from behind the cash register and made a beeline toward them. "Oh, I heard about this little sweetie pie. Hi, Levi!"

Levi buried his head in Jordan's shoulder and wailed. Jordan winced. "I'm sorry. He's found his voice and he's been using it. A lot."

"No, it's my fault. I always get excited and forget there's a reason our kids end up in our family. We're a little short on tables this morning, but Ash ran in for a cup of coffee and a Danish. He's in the back corner."

As she said the words, she tucked her hand through Jordan's arm and started walking.

"I don't want to disturb him. Really, Bertie, I can wait." A sense of desperation laced her voice. "We can get takeout!"

"Nonsense. He'll love the company." Bertie all but dragged Jordan to the corner table. "Look who's here to have breakfast with you, Ashley."

Ash's jaw clenched and Jordan smothered a laugh as she slid onto the seat. "Only a mother can get away with calling you by your full name."

Bertie chuckled. "I'll be right back with coffee for you and…chocolate milk for the little one?"

Jordan looked at Levi. "Sure, let's give it a try."

Ash was wearing khaki pants, a spotless white shirt and a bright green bow tie with blue whales. His black square-frame glasses should have made him look nerdy, but didn't. He just got cuter.

"Nice tie."

She was teasing him but he looked up from his Danish and said, "Thanks."

Catching the expression on her face, his eyes took on a knowing look. "Oh, you're joking. Hmm. It must only be the under-twelve set that likes dolphin-print bow ties."

He winked at Levi and a little pang hit her dead center in the belly. Why did he have to be so ridiculously handsome?

Their waitress, Lanna, placed a high chair at the end of the table and came back seconds later with a mug of coffee for Jordan. "The new baby's cute. What can I get you?"

"Blueberry pancakes, please. Nothing for Levi, here."

"Got it." Lanna ripped a ticket off and shoved the pad back in her pocket. She turned to Ash. "A refill for you, hot stuff?"

Ash cut his eyes at Lanna. "Such abuse. I'm leaving."

She was laughing under her breath as she walked to the kitchen to give Jordan's ticket to the cook.

"Lanna loves to rub that in my face." His cheeks turned ruddy. "When I was thirteen, I came in for a sandwich. She asked me what kind of bread I wanted and called me Ash, as she should. I said, 'that's "hot stuff" to you.'"

Jordan nearly spit out her coffee as she choked in laughter. "No wonder she gives you grief. You totally deserve it."

He laughed and slid a ten under the sugar dispenser. "I know. I'm not sure what I was thinking. I was barely five feet tall and a hundred pounds soaking wet."

"That's some confidence." She lifted baby Levi from the seat beside her into the high chair, but before she even got him seated, he was screaming. High-pitched, terrified screeching. She picked him up immediately, aware that every eye in the restaurant was on her.

Jordan pulled him into her arms and cuddled him as much as he would let her, saying over and over again into his ear, "You're okay, Levi. You're okay."

It wasn't long before the screams turned into sobs and then sniffles. He stuck his thumb in his mouth and closed his eyes tight against the world.

"Wow, when he found his voice, he really found it." A little shell-shocked, she sat back against the bench seat, hands shaking, her face flaming. "It didn't cross my mind that strapping him into the high chair would trigger the trauma for him."

Ash slid his glass of ice water to her. "You did exactly the right thing to handle it. He calmed down quickly. The pediatrician in me is impressed."

"I'm familiar with working with traumatized kids, just not usually this young. Being his foster mom makes it different than being a therapist, too."

"I've heard great things from my patients who are clients of yours."

She smiled. "You should come out some time and watch a session. The kids think they're just coming to ride, but they work hard. And honestly, there's something special about the horses. Some connection they have with kids with all kinds of special needs. I can't explain it, but it works."

"There's a huge need for people to have options for therapy. Not just kids, either. Don't give up."

"I won't. I'm not sure I could if I wanted to." Her therapy practice was her passion and she absolutely loved the work she did with the kids. She'd even coached a few adult PTSD survivors with good results.

"Don't give up with Levi, either. He's got a long way to go, but we'll get him there." Ash glanced at his watch and slid out of the booth. "I've got to run. My first patient will be waiting for me."

He took a few steps toward the door and turned back. "Hey, Jordan. Meltdowns happen. He learned during this one that you will be there for him when they do."

Touched, she nodded. To be honest, it was all she could do. She had no words. She watched Ash walk out of the restaurant, his characteristic confidence evident as he waved at Lanna and kissed his mom, stopping long enough to whirl her around until she swatted at him to put her down.

Lanna slid the blueberry pancakes onto the table, along with a pitcher of warm maple syrup. "Bless this baby's sweet heart. Yours, too. You stay as long as you like to finish that up."

"Thanks, Lanna."

Jordan leaned forward to take the first bite and nearly choked as someone popped into the seat across from her. A pretty blonde she recognized—from church, maybe?

"Hey, Jordan, I'm Darla. We met at the potluck after church a few weeks ago. I heard last night that you were picking this little one up and I called around. We've got meals planned for you for the next couple of weeks and Suzette Sloan pulled some baby supplies together for you. It's not much but would it be okay if she drops it off on your porch?"

Jordan's throat was full of unshed tears. She swallowed hard, focusing on the solid weight of little Levi in her arms. Meeting Darla's sparkling dark brown eyes, she smiled, willing her lips not to tremble. "I don't even know what to say. Y'all are so generous."

"You don't have to say anything—just say yes!" Darla laughed and pulled her cell phone out of her purse. "And give me your phone number in case we need to get in touch with you."

Jordan rattled it off as Darla typed it in. "What made you guys think about doing this?"

Darla tucked a loose curl behind her ear. "Well, to be honest, I think we all wish that we had the nerve to do what you guys are doing out there on the farm. Maybe someday." Darla's phone buzzed and she glanced at it before jumping to her feet. "I'm supposed to be at Clara's school right now. Okay, meals will start tonight and we'll just leave everything on your porch. I'll text you so you have my number."

As quick as she had arrived, Darla was gone. Jordan patted Levi on the back and decided to take her pancakes to go. She and Levi had to be at the WIC office in twenty minutes.

She glanced across the street at Ash's tidy office—with bright white paint and shiny black shutters. She wasn't really sure what to make of their newfound friendship, if it was friendship. They'd forged a kind of bond, by caring for Levi.

But maybe it was just that, a mutual concern for a sweet, sad baby boy.

Whatever. She had more important things on her mind than Ash Sheehan. Things like building her therapy practice and making sure Levi healed. She didn't have time to worry about Ash and their maybe-friendship. In fact, she was sure it wasn't anything at all.

And just to make sure she remembered that, she was going to stay as far away from the handsome doctor as possible.

When Jordan got home, Levi's caseworker was sitting on the porch steps with a file spread around her and a pencil between her teeth. Jordan had just spent three hours in the WIC office with a toddler who refused—understandably—to be strapped into a stroller. She was absolutely exhausted, and unlike her small charge, she couldn't take a nap on the drive home.

Bartlet nickered at her over the fence. The horses

were waiting for her. And so, apparently, was Reesa. Jordan hitched Levi higher on her hip and took a deep breath. "Hey, I didn't know you were coming this afternoon."

Reesa gathered the papers and pulled them into a stack. "I had to visit with the twins, Jamie and John, and Claire today, so I thought I'd drop in to see Levi, too. Save me a trip another day. How's he doing?"

Pushing open the door to the cottage, Jordan let the dog out and tried to remember if she'd left anything embarrassing on the floor. "Come on in."

She placed sleeping Levi on the crib mattress on the floor and went to the kitchen to pour two glasses of sweet tea, kicking a loose pair of socks under the couch as she went. "He hates the crib. We're working on it."

Reesa, in one of the chairs, waved a hand, dismissing it. "No worries. It takes time, sometimes more than you'd think, for them to adjust."

"Are we going to have a lot of time? Wait. Don't answer that. I know you don't have any way to really know." She held one of the glasses out to Reesa, with a napkin.

Reesa stuck a pencil into the pile of riotous curls on top of her head and leaned forward to take the glass. "Neither Mom nor Dad bonded out, so they're still in jail. I'm going to see them later this week to get some names of family from them. If they still won't give us anyone, we'll try to get the judge to compel them to, but we don't have a whole lot to hold over their heads. They're already facing significant time with the drug charges and the child endangerment."

"So we're probably looking at six months with Levi."

Reesa nodded, the colorful curls on her head bounc-

ing wildly. "At least. Levi will be classified medically
fragile and I have no idea what we'll find when we start
looking at family." She paused and, with her custom-
ary directness, added, "Do we need to find him another placement?"

"No." Jordan didn't hesitate. In just a couple of days,
Levi's journey had become inextricably entwined with
hers and she had to see it through with him. "He's just
starting to trust me. I'm not going to do that to him.
He has enough to deal with without me adding to it."

"Okay, good. Obviously, I think you're the perfect
person for him since you can help him with any kind of
physical or occupational therapy that he might need at
home." Reesa wrote something in her notes and looked
up again. "Now, let's talk about him. You said he hates
the crib. He will sleep out here, though?"

"Yes. I think it's the thing about being enclosed. He
freaks out in the car seat and high chair, too."

"Poor guy. How are his burns?"

"Better. I've been putting the cream on them and
they look less angry."

"If you can snap some pics and send them to me,
that would be good. I have the ones from the hospital,
but I'd like photos of his progress. Is he eating okay?"

"He won't eat solid food. I had a huge fight with
WIC today trying to get them to pay for formula for
a three-year-old. I'm going to have to get some docu-
mentation from the pediatrician that it's okay for Levi
to take a bottle, at least for now."

Reesa looked up. "That really cute pediatrician who
came with you to the hospital?"

"He didn't come with me." Jordan scowled. "He
met me there."

"Mmm-hmm. And what's going on with you two?"

"What? Nothing." Oh, man, she hoped that it wasn't that obvious that she was so unbelievably awkward around him. She twirled the end of one of her braids around her finger, let it go and then picked it up, wrapping it around her finger again. Then again, maybe she was just awkward in general. "Ash and I—we're just friends. His brother is married to my sister, that's all."

"He's really good-looking. Maybe you *should* start something." Reesa raised one perfectly manicured, pierced eyebrow.

Jordan sputtered out a laugh. "That's entirely inappropriate! And seriously, I'm not his type."

"Okay, I hear you." Reesa closed her notebook. "One last thing. I know Levi just got out of the hospital, but you'll need to make an appointment and get his intake form filled out by the superhot, there's-nothing-going-on-there Dr. Sheehan this week."

Jordan dug deep to find some peace and took a cleansing breath. She would make it work with her schedule. Somehow. "Of course."

"And now, I'm really sorry, but I have to see him awake while I'm here. Can you wake him up?"

"Yes. He's been sleeping a lot. He's healing, for one thing, but I'm not sure he had much restful sleep before. Let me get him a bottle before we wake him. He hasn't had anything in a couple of hours." In the kitchen, she got a bottle out of her new stash, quickly mixing six ounces of formula for Levi. "He's not always happy to see me, so I'm just warning you."

"You're doing a great job with him, Jordan. He's going to adjust. What are you going to do when you have to go back to work this week?"

"My hours are flexible and Claire has Mrs. Matthews, who's agreed to keep him during the day when I have clients. Unfortunately, it will be another adjustment for him." Jordan lifted Levi into her arms and tickled his foot to wake him up. He woke up scowling and opened his mouth to scream. She stuck the bottle in it.

Reesa laughed and gathered her stuff. "Good enough. You're a natural, but I guess you've had some practice with all of Claire's kids."

"I have. Will you keep me posted if there are any changes?"

"I'll do my best. And I'll see you next month if not before." Reesa let herself out the front door.

Jordan knew that Reesa meant well, but she also knew that information flowed slowly and usually in one direction in the system, from foster parent to caseworker, not the other way around. She looked into Levi's big brown eyes, which were focused on hers. "I guess we'll just have to wait and see. But you don't have to worry, buddy. We'll figure it out."

She hoped she was telling the truth. She prayed constantly for this sweet baby, who so did not deserve what had happened to him. *God, do Your will for him. Make it unmistakable.*

Her phone buzzed on the table beside her. A text from Reesa:

Don't forget about the pediatrician.

As if she could.

Chapter Four

Ash stopped at the reception desk. His nurse, Marissa, slid a file to the bottom of the stack on the counter. A grandmotherly woman with a heart of gold, she was the organizational glue that held his practice together. "We have a new patient. Levi Wheeler, three years old."

He glanced through the window into the waiting area and saw Jordan with Levi in her arms. He smiled. The other moms were dressed to the nines, having been taught from the cradle—according to his mother—not to leave the house without hair done and lipstick in place. Jordan was herself, boots and flannel, hair tied back, rebellious red curls framing her face. Levi had his head buried in her armpit. "Go ahead and put them in the red room."

"But—"

They were overbooked. They were *always* overbooked because who could turn away a sick kid? So they went in order of arrival. Sometimes, though, you had to break the rules. "Marissa, take a look at him."

His sweet nurse peeked over the counter and sighed. "Poor little one. He looks terrified."

"He's her new foster son. Let's get the two of them in a room." Ash stripped off his white lab coat and tossed it over a chair before picking up Levi's thin chart. He opened the door to the waiting room. "Ms. Conley?"

Jordan's eyes widened and darted around the room to the other moms, but she hastily made her way to the door. Jordan glanced out at the people lining the walls in the waiting room. "I think they're planning a mutiny. Might want to send out some snacks or something."

Ash laughed. "I'll take that under advisement. We thought waiting in a room might be more comfortable for Levi."

"You thought right. Thank you."

"Hey, buddy." Ash reached into his pocket for a sticker. He held it out to Levi, who looked at him from under Jordan's chin.

The little boy's eyes were huge in his thin face and seemed to question Ash's motives, but he stuck his hand out and took the sticker from Ash's hand. Ash considered that a victory. "You'll be waiting in the red room, better known as the Giraffe Room. I've got just a couple of patients to see before Levi, but I won't be long. Marissa?"

Ash's nurse showed Jordan to the red room and followed them in. After an eight-month-old with an ear infection and a two-year-old with eczema, Ash knocked on the door. He pushed it open to find that Jordan had sketched roads on the paper cover of the exam table and was showing Levi how to make sound effects for his Matchbox cars.

When the toddler saw Ash, he pulled his car close to his chest and narrowed his dark brown eyes.

Tucking the pen and extra cars back into the diaper bag, Jordan smiled at Levi. "It's okay, buddy. Dr. Sheehan is just going to give you a checkup. Remember how we watched the little girl give her stuffed animal a checkup on TV?"

"Time for a checkup, time for a checkup!" Ash sang the song from the kid's show.

Jordan laughed. "See, Levi? He even knows the song."

Ash pulled a couple more stickers out of his pocket, once again the pediatrician's secret weapon. He held them out to Levi. "We'll do as quick a check as possible today so I can fill out your form for the caseworker. I'm hoping he'll get used to me so he'll let me do a full exam soon without it being too traumatizing."

"What do you need me to do?"

"If you'll pick him up and put him on your shoulder, I'll look in his ears."

Jordan lifted Levi, and Ash took a peek in one ear and the other.

"Great job, Levi. Jordan, if you want to hold him in your lap with his back against your chest, I want to get a look in his throat and nose. I'll try to be fast."

Jordan held Levi's arms and hands still and Ash took a quick look in the little guy's nose. Just as he was gearing up to yell, Ash got a look in his throat. "All done. Let's put him on the table and we'll see how far we can get with an exam. I want to check those burns if he'll let me."

She laid Levi on the table and Ash held his exam light up, pretending to blow it out. No laughs, but at least he got a little smile from the somber little boy.

He gently checked one fragile arm and then the other. The burns looked better.

A quick check of reflexes and he would call it a day. Ash slid his thumbnail up the sole of Levi's foot. His big toe curved back and his toes spread. Babinski in a three-and-a-half-year-old?

He tested the other foot. The primitive reflex was not as strong, but it was still there. With long practice, Ash hid his concern, smiling at Levi. "You did awesome, little man!"

"So, rainbow fingernails are in now?" Jordan pulled a T-shirt over Levi's head.

Ash glanced down at his hands and yes, his fingernails were painted in rainbow pastel shades. His face flushed hot, but he laughed and shrugged. "It's the latest thing, didn't you know? I have a little patient going through chemo right now. She has specialists overseeing her care, but when I can, I go by to see her. Last night she was bored and her mom needed a nap, hence my new fashion statement."

Jordan's eyes were soft. "I'm sorry. That must hit home for you."

"It does, a little," he admitted. "And she's a real sweetheart of a kid. I hate it for her. You ready?"

She pulled some soft knit pants over Levi's scrawny legs and picked him up. "Now I am."

"Good. I want to run a few tests on Levi. Because he's so small and isn't crawling or walking, I want to rule out some more serious issues. Marissa will call you once the appointments are set up, okay?"

Jordan stopped halfway out the door. "Should I be worried?"

He smiled into her already very concerned eyes. "Not yet. I'll tell you when to worry. I promise."

She nodded. "It's just— He's been through a lot, you know?"

"I do know." Ash opened the door because feelings were churning in his chest. He saw dozens of patients every day and never had he wanted to take one of the mothers in his arms and reassure her that everything would be okay. He cleared his throat. "Jordan, I promise we're going to take good care of him."

He watched as she walked down the hall toward the reception area, her red head bent toward a dark, curly one.

"Doc?" Marissa shook his arm, startling him. "You have a patient waiting in two."

"Right. I need to make some notes first. And I want you to go ahead and make an appointment for a CT scan for Levi—spine and hips." Marissa noted his request and walked away. He stood there a second longer.

Jordan was so different from other girls—women— he'd known. She hadn't had an easy time of it but she wasn't waiting for life to come to her. Instead, she took life by the reins, making it be what she wanted it to be. There was a part of him that deeply desired that kind of determination and definitely admired it.

He called after her, "Jordan!"

She turned back and he was at her side in a second, before he had time to think about it, consider the consequences.

"Go out with me. Dinner on Friday?"

Jordan stared into his eyes as if scrutinizing his motives and he wondered what she thought she saw there. He didn't even know what his motives were.

After a long minute, when every eye in the place seemed to be trained on him, she said, "No, thank you."

No, thank you. That was what you say when someone offers you Brussels sprouts and you hate them, not what you say when someone you like invites you to dinner.

Over the rushing in his ears, he heard her say a few more words, and then over it all, the sound of an infant screaming in the room to his left.

Marissa put a merciful hand on his arm. "Room two is waiting, Dr. Sheehan."

He turned and went to the door of the exam room. With his hand on the doorknob, he stopped. Struggling to come up with appropriate words, he finally said, "Okay, then, I'll see you around."

Color high in her cheeks, Jordan nodded and fled.

A week later Jordan was still thinking about that moment. He'd closed in on her with long strides, blue eyes smiling at her, those tiny crinkles in the corners. Stupid rainbow fingernails, making her feel all warm and mushy about him.

In her mind, when he'd asked her to go to dinner, she didn't blurt out that he wasn't her type. She didn't even hesitate. She smiled slowly up at him and said, *What took you so long?* Or *That sounds like fun.*

Was that so hard?

She scowled and shoveled fresh pellets into Bartlet's stall. "Yes, thank you, that sounds like fun." See, how hard was that?

"Who are you talking to?"

She went still. She knew that deep voice. Slowly, she turned around, her cheeks burning. Ash leaned on the door to the barn, a bakery bag dangling from his relaxed fingers. He was absolutely spotless, as usual. Nary a crease would dare to mar his perfect khakis.

Did the man never get thrown up on? He was a pediatrician.

In contrast, she was dressed—as usual—in riding pants and flannel. She had mud down her side where one of her young clients used her hip as a stepstool getting off his horse after therapy.

And she had been talking to herself. *About him.*

She stood the shovel on end and raised one eyebrow. "I'm a very good conversationalist, I'll have you know."

"Apparently." He pushed off the wall with his shoulder and held out the bag. "For you. Double chocolate. Jules said it was your favorite."

"It is. And you have perfect timing, actually. I'm done here. Want to share? I have milk." When he gave her a look, she laughed. "No worries. We ate earlier because Levi can't hold out until I'm finished with the animals. His babysitter—actually, your sister Wynn—is putting him to bed. He's finally able to sleep in his room and even goes into his crib without crying."

She slid the barn door closed and locked it.

"You don't have to put the horses in?" He followed her down the trail around the pond toward her home.

"It's warm enough now that I let them stay in the field sometimes. They work hard during the day, so they frolic at night." Her lips twitched at her horse humor. See, she was funny. She could carry on a conversation. Reaching her front porch, she sat on the small bench outside the front door and shucked her boots, entering the cottage in sock feet, Ash right behind her. "Hey, Wynn, how did he do?"

Ash's sister Wynn put her finger to her lips. "Sound asleep. That last bottle did the trick."

"He didn't sleep long this afternoon. I figured he'd go down pretty easy." Gus nosed his way out of Levi's room and ambled over, bumping his head against her hand until she crouched down to give him her attention. She looked up at Wynn as she scratched behind Gus's ears. "Did he eat any food?"

"A few crackers and some mandarin oranges, even swallowed a little bit." Wynn pulled the ponytail holder out of her long blond hair, shaking it out to fall down her back. "He's precious. What time do you need me tomorrow?"

"My clients are in the morning tomorrow, so Mrs. Matthews can watch him. Thanks, though. You're a lifesaver."

"Pish." Wynn picked up her purse, a small suede satchel with six-inch fringe, as she walked to the door. "I love that little guy."

Ash towered over his petite sister. He put his arm around her. "If you're looking for something to do while you're home, I could use some help in the office. My receptionist is on maternity leave as of Tuesday."

Wynn gave her brother a light shove. "Good luck with that."

He closed the door behind Wynn. "She's always been mean to me."

"I can't understand why. I know you're glad to see her. She said she hasn't been home for more than a day or two in three years." Jordan grinned and held up the bakery bag, thankful that no awkwardness lingered between them. "Want a piece of the cupcake?"

He smiled. "There's an oatmeal cookie in there for me. I was hoping we could talk for a minute."

Unease drilled her right in the belly, but she poured two big glasses of cold milk and placed the cupcake on a napkin. "Let's go sit in the living room and I'll light a fire."

With a long match from the container on the mantel, she lit the tinder under the logs. After watching a few seconds to make sure it caught, she joined Ash on the floor behind the coffee table. Gus settled beside her, his big head in her lap. "You don't really strike me as a sit-on-the-floor-and-eat-cookies kind of guy."

He looked up, surprised. "Really? At home, I always eat cookies on the floor."

She laughed. "Okay, okay."

The cupcake was her favorite but she couldn't eat it, not knowing that Ash wanted to talk about Levi. "So what's going on?"

Ash picked up the cookie and put it down again without taking a bite. "Okay. Let's start at the beginning. We know that Levi is developmentally delayed. Trauma can do that. Neglect can do that. But when I examined him, he had a reflex—the Babinski reflex—that should be gone by the time he's three. Sometimes if a child still has that reflex later, it's a sign that there might be nerve damage. Because of the nature of the abuse that he suffered, I felt like it would be better to do the tests and find out for sure."

"You sound like you're reading from a report."

He made a face. "Sorry. Professional hazard. I usually do better."

She threaded her fingers into Gus's thick pelt, letting the familiarity of his soft fur soothe her. "It's okay.

So the tests that we had done were to see if he has nerve damage. Like to his spine?"

"Yes. The fact that he isn't crawling or walking even though his nutrition is better and he's getting stronger made me wonder if his condition is irreversible."

Jordan couldn't breathe. "And the results of the test?"

"They were inconclusive." His eyes were on hers, and the concern in them was so deep that it made her feel exposed, like he could see how shattered she was at the thought that Levi might have suffered permanent damage at the hands of his parents.

She swallowed hard, trying to process but knowing that she couldn't really do that until she had some space to grieve. "So what you're saying is that he may never walk?"

He stared at the fire for a second before he answered, meeting her eyes again. "I'm saying it's a possibility. Kids' bodies heal differently than adults. We just don't know—won't know—until we know."

Burying her face in her hands, she tried so hard to fight back the emotional response to what he had told her and just look at it logically. She couldn't. Silent sobs racked her body as she tried in vain to just take in a breath. How cruel was it that the abuse he had suffered strapped in a chair and left there could consign him to a wheelchair permanently?

Slowly, she became aware of Ash's arms around her, his lips murmuring against her hair. "It's gonna be okay."

She pushed away from him, scrubbing the tears from her cheeks. "I'm so sorry. I don't know what—I hate to cry."

"You love him. That's understandable."

"He's not even my kid." She drew in a long, shaky breath. "And somehow that makes it even worse. He deserves a happy, stable life after all he's been through and I have no way of making sure that happens."

"I know. He does deserve that." He rubbed his temples with his long doctor fingers and she noted that his fingernails were no longer rainbow, but there was a smudge of pink polish on one nail.

She felt a pang somewhere in the region of her heart as she thought about the fact that he took time to do manicures with little girls with cancer. Maybe he wasn't quite the playboy that she made him out to be in her mind. He'd also taken the time to come here and talk through this with her because he knew it would be difficult.

She took another deep breath and tried to focus. Okay, so Levi might be in a wheelchair. At the very least, this information meant that he needed physical therapy immediately. It would be a long, arduous road for him, and she hated that thought. "Is it painful?"

"His legs? I don't think so. He doesn't act like it is. And he does have at least some feeling in his legs. My recommendation would be to do intense physical therapy and reevaluate in six months. There's a doctor in Atlanta who has done some pretty great work with injuries of this kind, too. It would be good to get a second opinion. I'm not a specialist."

"It's going to be hard."

"Yes." He paused. "No doubt about that—it will be hard, on both of you."

"I've done hard things before." Claire had been working full-time when their mom was diagnosed with pancreatic cancer. It had been quick and it had been brutal and, while they shared the responsibility, it had been Jordan who had been at their mother's side.

"When I think about the things in my life that shaped my character the most, it isn't the things that came easily to me that I remember." Ash made a face. "Sounds like a cliché when I say it like that, but it's not."

She nodded her head slowly. "It really doesn't matter how it affects me. I'm an adult and I may not have known what we were facing, but I signed up for this. He didn't."

The fire had burned down to embers. Ash looked at his watch and grimaced. "I should go. I have a patient having her tonsils out in the morning and I promised I'd be there before she goes in for surgery."

He got to his feet and tousled her hair slightly. "It's gonna be okay. You don't have to do this alone. We'll all be here to help."

Once again, Jordan, who hated to cry, had tears pooling in her eyes. She nodded, not trusting herself to speak. She heard the door open and looked back. "Hey, Ash."

When he turned around, she said, "Ask me again sometime."

"Ask you wh— Oh." He grinned, that all-American smile of his flashing white in the dim room. "Maybe when my pride recovers."

The door closed behind him before she could think of a clever retort. He was so confusing to her. She knew him to be a good-time guy, never serious about anything except maybe medicine. Now that she was spending more time with him, she was seeing a sweet, more sensitive side. She couldn't help but wonder which one was the real Ash Sheehan.

* * *

Ash walked slowly around the pond toward his car. The stars were so bright out here, even just a couple of miles from town. The black sky was vast and it seemed like it should be quiet, but it wasn't. Horses blowing, donkeys shuffling, wind whispering in the tops of the pines and the occasional shout of a child who was supposed to be asleep.

It was peaceful, even with his mind on a special little boy with a very special foster mom.

"Nice night for a walk?"

The voice startled his heart into double time until he realized it was his brother, Joe, sitting in the dark on the back porch of the farmhouse. He walked a little closer. "A little chilly, to be honest. What are you doing?"

"Having my celebratory bedtime root beer. Want one?"

Ash shrugged. "Sure."

When Joe came back from the kitchen, Ash took the cold amber bottle and smiled. "You got the good stuff."

"Yes, well, by this time of day, I feel the need to treat myself." Joe took a swig, wiped his mouth with the back of his hand and said, "So what's going on with Jordan?"

"I don't know what you mean."

Joe pierced Ash with a look from his ice-blue eyes. "You have a reputation with the ladies. Nothing wrong with that—until you set your sights on my sister-in-law."

"I...umm...I don't have my sights set on anyone. If you must know, I asked her out and she turned me down."

"Great. Now you'll see her as a challenge."

"I won't. I don't, Joe. I like her. She's different than the women I date. We're friends, I think."

"You *think*?" In the relative darkness of the porch with only the glow from the kitchen windows for light, Joe's glower was still spectacular.

"Do they teach you to do that in cop school or were you just blessed to be able to use that look at will?" Ash grinned. "I'm kidding. Yes, we're friends. I'm her foster son's pediatrician, that's all."

Joe drained the last of his root beer and set the bottle down none too gently. "If you should happen to change your mind about that, don't."

"I'll consider that carefully." Ash handed Joe his own empty bottle and walked down the steps. "You know, I'm not as shallow as you think, Joe."

"I don't think you're shallow, but your relationships usually are. Jordan deserves better."

As he walked to his car, slightly irritated by his older brother's characterizations, he had to admit that Joe was right. His relationships usually were shallow by design.

And Jordan did deserve better than him.

Chapter Five

Jordan pulled the body brush out of her grooming kit and went to work brushing off the dirt and dust she'd loosened with the curry comb. She had Leo tied off on one side of the barn door while Amelia worked on Freckles on the other side. During the week, the volunteers who came in to assist with clients did the daily grooming before tacking up. They were awesome, but she wanted her own hands on her horses at least once a week. She was the one who knew them best and she could recognize a little problem before it became a big problem.

Joe's daughter, Amelia, laughed as Freckles's tail smacked her in the back. Again. "I really think he does that on purpose."

"He definitely does." Jordan scraped a stubborn mud spot off Leo's shoulder. "He thinks it's hilarious to grab the end of my braids. We should've named him Rascal."

Sundays had become—hands down—Jordan's favorite time of the week at Red Hill Farm. Since they got their first foster crew in, Claire had insisted they have family dinners on the lawn after church. Every

Sunday the family gathered and ate together on the long row of picnic tables. When it was cold, they had a fire. When it rained, they ate inside in all the nooks and crannies of the old plantation house.

Most of the time the spread was a hodgepodge of makings for sandwiches fruit, and whatever anyone else wanted to bring. Sometimes they had a lot of green bean casseroles, but the point wasn't the food.

It was being together.

Over the last few months, as foster children had come and gone, their families had been included in Sunday family dinner, too. It wasn't unusual to see a birth family sitting with a foster family. Black, white, grandparents, young parents. In Jordan's mind, it was a picture of what a table in Heaven would look like.

Church, family, horses, perfect.

"Can I help?" One of Claire and Joe's younger ones, a tiny six-year-old named Penny, stood at the fence. Behind Penny, Jordan could see a group of kids around Ash, who had brought his guitar and had them squealing with laughter at his silly songs.

She smiled at Penny. "How about I finish up with Leo here and then we bring Hagrid out for a ride? He could really use the exercise."

Penny nodded, big brown eyes wide on Jordan's face. A month ago those eyes wouldn't even connect, the trauma she'd experienced evident in every inch of her. Narrow shoulders had curved in as if to protect herself from some potential attempt to steal more of her childhood. And Jordan was reminded again that the children at Red Hill Farm weren't a distraction, they were the *reason* they did this.

Penny's eyes were still on Jordan, taking everything in.

Jordan held up the tool she was using. "This pick cleans Leo's feet so that his hooves stay strong and healthy."

Scraping the dirt and muck out of Leo's hooves, she checked for any sores, cracks or infection. She'd been Penny once, a long time ago, just wanting to be close to the horses. "See how easy that is? But remember that Leo is used to me. He's been my horse for a long time, so he's comfortable with me around his feet. Even so, I still put my hand on him when I'm moving around so he knows where I am when he can't see me."

"Always stay back unless you are with a grown-up." Penny parroted Jordan's most often repeated phrase.

"That's right. That's the number one rule around the horses. Go get your helmet on. I'm almost done with Leo." She ran a soft microfiber cloth over Leo's hair to get the last of the dust. Taking a minute to scratch his face and ears, she gave him some sweet talk before taking him back to his stall in the barn.

She returned to the paddock area leading Hagrid, the Haflinger pony. With his long blond mane and fuzzy body, he looked like a big stuffed animal. Even the kids who started out afraid of horses usually liked Hagrid. She tied him up next to Freckles and lifted Penny onto the pony's broad back.

"You ready?" She clucked to Hagrid and they walked together around the pen. "Just relax and let your body move with Hagrid. There you go. You're doing great being the boss of you!"

For fifteen minutes she took Hagrid around the ring, giving Penny simple commands. "Stretch forward with both arms and pat both sides of Hagrid's neck."

Penny nodded, her concentration evident. The little tasks weren't difficult but helped with confidence on the horse, strengthened her core muscles and gave a squirmy six-year-old all kinds of sensory input. "Put your arms over your head and wiggle your fingers like you're tickling the clouds."

Penny giggled.

When they reached the fence nearest the house, Hagrid stopped. "Great job! High five?"

Penny flashed a brilliant smile at Jordan and slapped hands before swinging her leg over Hagrid's back and sliding to the ground. The little girl patted the pony on the neck and gave him a kiss on the side of his nose. Hagrid turned his fuzzy face toward her and blew gently.

"Hagrid is the best pony ever." Penny threw her arms around Jordan and squeezed. "I love you, Aunt J."

Jordan's free arm slid around the slim shoulders and squeezed. "I love you, too, Penny."

As her foster niece—was that even a thing?—dashed out of the corral into the yard, Jordan called after her. "Don't forget to hang your helmet in the tack room!"

She noticed Ash leaning on the fence, his guitar at his side, a speculative look in his eyes. "What?"

"A month ago when Penny came in for her first checkup, she would barely look up when someone talked to her. She's made huge progress."

"Red Hill Farm." She shrugged. How the combo of love and safety and animals worked together in such synergy couldn't really be explained in words.

He smiled, his dimples deepening in his cheeks, and her heart took a little tumble. Why did he have to be so darned good-looking?

"Give me a tour. Show me."

She paused in the middle of lifting the saddle from

Hagrid's back. "What do you mean? You know this place as well as anyone."

"Not from your perspective."

Amelia reached for the lead rope. "I'll brush Hagrid for you, Aunt Jordan."

She still hesitated. She had a toddler to think about now, but when she glanced over, he was sound asleep in his Pack 'n Play next to Mrs. Matthews, who was reading a paperback. "I guess I've got a few minutes. Walk or ride?"

"You have a four-wheeler?"

"I have a horse. A few of them."

Ash made a face. "I'm embarrassed to admit this but I'm not much for horses. They have big teeth and they always look like they want to kick me."

"Well, I think we'll start with the horses, then. Amelia and I usually give them a thorough grooming on Sunday, mainly because we like to spend the time with them. Otherwise volunteers do it."

"Do the people in therapy ever groom them?"

"Sometimes. The teenagers like to help care for them." She stopped at the first stall and Bartlet stuck his gray head over the railing. "This big baby is Bartlet. He had a long career as a jumper and was a champion. He's twenty-two now and completely unflappable. Nothing bothers him."

"He's enormous." Ash lingered near the wall farthest from Bartlet.

"One of the reasons horses are so good at therapy is that they respond to our emotions. It doesn't mean he'll freak out or anything, but it's kind of like with kids when they come into your office. They feel out of control and want to know who's in charge. Rub his neck. Take a deep breath and be confident with him and he'll respond to that."

Ash cut his blue eyes at her. "I'm confident that he outweighs me by a thousand pounds or so."

But he stepped forward and gave Bartlet a short but solid rub on the neck. Bartlet, being Bartlet, was a perfect gentleman.

Jordan walked to the next stall. "This handsome guy is Leo. He was my first therapy horse. He's sturdy and sweet, a favorite with the kids."

Leo nudged her with his big brown head and she scratched his favorite spot under his forelock, right at the top of his distinctive white blaze. When Ash stepped closer, she showed him how to rub under the mane. Entwining her fingers into his, she slid their hands together down Leo's neck. She did this exact thing with kids all the time, but with Ash, somehow it felt…intimate.

Her breath caught.

He turned his head and his eyes locked on hers. "Jordan…"

Heartbeat rushing in her ears, she moved her hand. "You try it."

She saw the deep breath he drew, but he followed her lead. "Like this?"

Leo bobbed his head. Jordan laughed. "Yes, exactly. It's good to keep one hand on his neck and rub or groom with the other. It lets the horse know where you are and also gives you the opportunity to push back if he gets frisky."

Ash laughed softly. "Okay. Not worried about that at all."

"Don't be. We teach safety rules, but kids are unpredictable, and some of our clients make erratic movements. We couldn't have a horse that was intolerant of that kind of thing. So, you know, you should be fine."

She turned, not realizing he was right behind her. His hands closed around her arms, his eyes searching hers, and she knew she wasn't getting away with a distraction this time.

A smile played around his lips. "I don't feel very safe. My heart's beating too fast and I want to run away, but the adrenaline tells me to stay and see what happens. Do you want to see what happens, Jordan?"

His hand slid into her hair and her lips parted. "Ash."

The barn door banged open. Jordan jumped back, slamming her elbow on Leo's stall door. One of the twins poked his head into the corridor. "Aunt J, Mrs. Matthews said to tell you that Levi is awake and hungry."

"I'm on my way." She rubbed her elbow and winced, following the ten-year-old scamp out the door. She glanced back to see Ash leaning on the wall across from Leo, his hand in his hair, eyes closed.

She didn't know what had been about to happen between them, but a kind of weird electricity had been in the air. She just knew she didn't have time for it. Or patience, really. Ash had his own set of rules about relationships and she was pretty sure that they weren't anything like hers.

Maybe he saw her as a challenge, or maybe he genuinely liked her. It didn't really matter. He was a good guy, but trying to be more than friends would be a huge mistake.

Ash paused briefly outside the exam room door to glance at the file in his hand. Claire and the two youngest were here for a recheck on their last ear infections. He was reasonably sure that Georgia, who was two, was going to need tubes in her ears before it was over. He knocked gently and pushed open the door to the exam room—slowly, so as not to knock over any toddler who might be playing behind the door.

"Hey, guys!" He pulled a sticker out of his pocket for each of the kids. Start with the bribe, he figured, and the kids would be preoccupied for at least a few minutes.

Claire stood like a goalie in front of the examining table, ready to stop an infant or toddler from launching herself onto the floor. "About time you got here. We've been in the room for forty-five minutes. Forty-five minutes, Ash. Do you know what it's like being in a six-by-six room with these two for forty-five minutes?"

"Yikes. Sorry." He placed the earpieces for his stethoscope in his ear. "I had a four-month-old come in with bronchiolitis. We tried some breathing treatments but ended up having to admit him."

Claire sighed. "I've been working up a good head of steam for half an hour now and you go and have a good reason for running behind."

He paused in listening to Georgia's lungs and shot Claire a sideways glance. "Usually do. She sounds much better than she did last time you were here. Let's check her ears."

"So I hear you've been hanging out with Jordan quite a bit."

"I already had this talk with Joe. I have no intentions toward your sister." He spoke without looking up.

"What? I don't care about that. You should be asking her out, you dope."

"I love it that we're so close you feel you can insult me in my office." His tone was dry. He had two sisters who loved to annoy him, and Claire made three.

He finished with Georgia's ears. The left eardrum was still red and sluggish.

Claire handed Georgia her phone and picked Sweetness up. She'd been here so much in the last few months that she didn't even need coaching through the process. He put the stethoscope on the five-month-old's chest, then listened to her back. "They both sound better. Good job, Mom."

"They're both sleeping again, so I figured. So, did you tell Jordan?"

Inches from Claire's face as he looked in the ears of her youngest foster baby, Ash said absently, "Tell her what?"

Claire sighed. "About Victoria."

He stopped, his fingers going cold. He drew in a deep breath and prayed for patience. "Joe needs to learn to keep his mouth shut."

"We're married. There are no secrets." Claire flipped Sweetness to her other shoulder so Ash could look in the other ear. "I just think Jordan would understand why you haven't settled down with one person if you explain about Victoria."

Ash looked in Sweetness's other ear, eardrum pink and vibrating normally. "It was a long time ago. There's nothing to tell."

Claire hitched the baby higher on her hip. "Then why haven't you asked Jordan out? I know you like her."

He shook his head. She was such a fixer. She and Joe were together and now she wanted everyone else to be just as happy as they were. And if she could, she would take every child in Alabama who needed a home.

Well, he was perfectly happy the way he was.

He liked his life.

Except, did he? "I asked her out and she said no."

"See?" Claire demanded, digging in the diaper bag with one hand and coming up with a sippy cup for Georgia.

"See what? She doesn't want to go on a date and I respect that. We're friends." An image popped into his brain of the moment in the barn with electricity nearly popping between them. If one of the twins hadn't come in, he knew he would have kissed Jordan. And she would have kissed him back.

"Just explain to her that your heart was broken and you've been grieving."

"I love you like a sister, Claire. You know I do. But you're getting close to the line."

Her eyes softened. "I'm sorry. I love you both and I want you to be happy."

"You're going to have to let each of us figure that out in our own way, kiddo." He typed in the script for Georgia and sent it to the pharmacy. "I sent a prescription for a different antibiotic for Georgia. That ear still isn't healed up. I want to see her in two weeks and if it's not better, I'm referring you to the ENT."

"She's supposed to go to her biological aunt next week, but I'll make sure the caseworker knows." Claire handed him the baby and gathered all the books, broken crayons, sippy cups and toys that had scattered all over the small exam room, shoving them into her enormous bag.

She took Sweetness back and grabbed Georgia by the hand. "Thanks, Ash. I'm sorry if I was meddling."

He opened the door for them, laughing. "If?"

"I'm meeting Jordan for lunch at the Hilltop in a few minutes. Tuesday's our day because she doesn't have midday clients. You should join us."

She just couldn't help it. She had to interfere. "I'm sorry, Claire. I have a drug rep bringing lunch in for the staff."

He watched her leave and then told his nurse, Marissa, he needed a quick break. He went into the private bathroom next to his office and leaned over the sink, his stomach churning. Splashing cold water on his face didn't help much. He stared at himself in the mirror, but what he saw wasn't the healthy image of himself that he usually saw. It was the image of himself as a sick little boy. Thin face, pallid skin, dark circles under his eyes.

He and Victoria met when they were both little kids in the hospital. With IV poles in hands and masks covering their faces, together they'd terrorized the hospital staff. Two little monkeys wearing masks, his mother used to say.

They were soul mates, able to understand what the other one was thinking without saying a word. They had stayed in contact over the years, their mothers making sure they got to see each other often. When Ash spent two weeks in the hospital in ninth grade, Victoria only left his side to go to school. In eleventh grade, her Hodgkin's recurred. There was chemo, radiation, surgery, a failed bone marrow transplant.

And Victoria died.

Twelve years later it still took his breath away to think about it.

Maybe Claire was right. Maybe his resistance to settling down with anyone and only dating people who were unlikely to mean anything to him had to do with losing Victoria. But the fact was, he'd had cancer, too. It was horrible and painful and he remembered it so clearly, even though he'd been a little boy. But all he'd gone through with cancer was *nothing* compared to the pain of losing Victoria.

Maybe it was selfish or maybe he was being selfless, he didn't know. He only knew he didn't want to do to anyone else, ever, what happened to him when Victoria died. A part of him had died, too.

In the mirror, his eyes were dark. In these moments he saw himself too clearly. He wasn't the pediatrician that the kids loved and the moms had a crush on. He wasn't the singer of silly songs. He was the lone survivor of a relationship that had been the world to him.

And to this day, he hadn't figured out how to live with that.

Chapter Six

Chores on a farm never ended. Jordan had the tack laid out on the fence line and a couple of sawhorses she'd found in the barn. Normally, cleaning and oiling the saddles and other riding equipment wasn't something they had to do often, but with so many riders and so many horses, it was important they keep their tack in good condition.

Levi was on a quilt in the grass under the oak tree. She could easily see and hear him, but at the moment he was lying on his back, looking at the dappled light in the canopy of the big tree.

She was cleaning some pieces today, and some that she washed yesterday, she was oiling today. Dirty, stiff leather became shiny, supple leather through a very simple process. The task was remarkably enjoyable, probably because there was immediate gratification, something that didn't happen often when therapy was your deal.

Claire and Joe's kids were trickling out of the house as they finished their homework, the older kids to weed and water the soon-to-be garden and the younger ones to the playground equipment. Claire was probably in the kitchen feeding the little ones. Her enormous seventeen-passenger van was parked in the driveway.

Amelia came running out of the house, jumped the steps, landed on the grass and did a forward roll. "Aunt Jordan, can I help? I have thirty minutes before I have to start feeding."

"Of course." She handed Amelia a rag. Each of the kids had at least one job—the garden, the animals, the dishes, folding clothes. Some of it depended on their strengths, and some of it depended on how heavy their academic load was, or their own responsibilities. Kiera, the only teenager they had right now besides Amelia, had her own baby.

Jordan checked on Levi, who had rolled onto his tummy and was watching the baby goats playing nearby. One of the kids must have left the door to the barn open again. The goats had their own pasture with much better fencing than the pasture the horses roamed in, but they were escape artists, often aided by the children.

"I have a test tomorrow. I hate algebra." Amelia scowled at the bridle as she rubbed oil into it.

Jordan buffed the saddle to a shine and stepped back to look at it. "I always hated it in school, too, but I use it all the time. How do you think I figure out what ratios go in the feed for the animals?"

"I didn't say I didn't know it. I just said I hate it. There's a difference." Amelia flipped her long dark hair over one shoulder.

"Point taken." Jordan laughed. "I'm glad to hear it. You can help me next time."

From the yard, she heard a hoarse sound, almost

like someone clearing his throat. She looked up to see Wendy, one of the baby goats, had ventured onto the quilt with Levi.

The little goat nibbled at Levi's hair and he swatted at it with hands that were just beginning to fill out. Wendy bounded away and then slowly crept back to nibble at his hair again. Again, Levi waved his hands in the air and Wendy bounded away before coming back to nibble at Levi with her soft goat lips.

Jordan started over to shoo Wendy away but she heard the hoarse noise again. She stopped to watch the game. Levi reached for the goat, Wendy bounded away and Levi *laughed*.

She cried.

It was the first sign, the very first real sign, that Levi was beginning to heal. Slowly, Jordan joined them, so as not to scare the baby or the goat. She lay down on the quilt beside Levi and he turned his face to hers. Those beautiful big brown eyes were smiling at her. He giggled and pointed at Wendy. "Goat."

She had to swallow hard to talk past the lump in her throat but she nodded. "Yes, goat. Wendy is a silly little goat."

Thank You, God. Thank You that this sweet baby is learning to trust again. Learning to heal.

The feed bucket clanged in the barn and Wendy heard it, too. She trotted toward the barn and her dinner, the game with Levi forgotten.

Jordan sat up and held her hands out to Levi. "Come on, buddy, let's go see Aunt Claire. I can't wait to tell her you said a word! Smart boy!"

As she lifted him up, she wondered how many other words were locked away in that little brain of his, waiting to be released. He was growing, too, a good three or four pounds heavier and two inches taller than he'd been when he first came a couple of weeks ago.

The speech therapist told her that as Levi started to trust the new world he was living in, his speech would develop because some of the brain space he'd been using for survival would be freed up for actual learning and development.

She ran for the house and he giggled some more as he bounced along. What a sweet breakthrough! There were many more hurdles to come for Levi, she knew, but wow, she would take the victories when they came.

Jordan took the stairs, dodging Penny, who was playing with a My Little Pony toy and one of the twins, who had Spiderman. Penny looked up. "Aunt J, Spiderman wants to ride My Little Pony to the police headquarters. Do you think she should give him a ride?"

After a few seconds of serious thought, Jordan nodded. "Yes, I think My Little Pony would like to help Spiderman catch the bad guys."

A grin spread across Penny's face. "I think so, too!"

Jordan pushed open the door to Claire's kitchen. Mrs. Matthews was at the stove. Claire, wearing a mint-green tunic and leggings, was at the island feeding puffs to Sweetness. Sitting across from her, a coffee mug in front of him and a serious expression on his face, was Ash.

She stopped short. Levi caught sight of Mrs. Matthews and bounced in Jordan's arms. "Cookie!"

Everyone stared. Claire grinned. "Did he just say a word?"

"Yes!" Jordan handed Levi to Mrs. Matthews, who

was only too happy to oblige him with a cookie. "And he said *goat* a minute ago!"

She poured herself a glass of lemonade from the pitcher on the island and scooched onto a stool. "What's going on? I don't like that expression, Ash."

He didn't say anything. Claire didn't, either, actually. She was staring out the window over the sink, her hand curved protectively around her rapidly expanding waistline.

A knot settled in the pit of Jordan's stomach. "Guys. Seriously. What's going on?"

Ash cleared his throat. "This morning a child came into the clinic with fever and a rash. These are common in childhood diseases and, at first, I wasn't worried about it at all, but her fever was very high and her eyes were red and sensitive to the light."

"What are you saying?"

"She has measles, Jordan." He reached for her hand and slid his fingers through hers. "She's in the hospital in isolation now."

"Well, that's no big deal, right? Aren't most people vaccinated?"

"Most people are. Unless they are immune compromised, or, in some cases, neglected."

She searched out Claire's eyes. "Like our kids."

"Yes, mine are vaccinated now, but Sweetness isn't old enough yet."

The implication of what Ash was saying was sinking in. It was as if her heart didn't want to accept what her brain already knew. Her fingers tightened around his. "Levi isn't vaccinated yet, either, that we know of. We were waiting until he was stronger. And because he wasn't going to day care, it wasn't a big deal."

Ash's blue eyes were rarely without a twinkle. He had laugh lines for a reason, his easygoing nature perfect for pediatrics. But he wasn't laughing now. "Jordan…"

"Have people in town been exposed?" Was that what this was about? She was going to have to keep Levi isolated for a while? She reached for her baby, and Mrs. Matthews transferred him back to her, crumbs and all.

Ash drew in a quiet breath, but his free hand was fisted against his khaki-clad thigh. "They were all over town. The mom thought her toddler had a cold until her fever shot up. They ate lunch at the Hilltop on Tuesday."

He waited and watched her face. She wondered why until what he'd said sank in.

"Tuesday?" She was off the stool and at Claire's side in point-two seconds. "We were at the Hilltop for lunch on Tuesday."

Claire nodded. "I know."

Jordan turned to Ash, the toddler on her hip. "Isn't there a shot or something you can give us?"

He shook his head. "You have to give the vaccine in the first 72 hours after exposure and we passed that some hours ago. I think we're going to have to wait it out. The incubation period is seven to twenty-one days. You and Claire will have to be vigilant."

"Wait. Claire, what about the baby? Isn't measles supposed to be really dangerous for unborn babies?"

Claire put her hand on Jordan's arm. "It's okay. I should be covered. I had a booster before I started working as a caseworker."

"Ash?" Jordan needed confirmation that her twin

sister would be safe, and put her own hand on her sister's belly bump.

"She's going to be fine and our little niece or nephew will be protected by her antibodies." He stood. "I have to go. I have other patients who were exposed. They'll need to be monitored and I want to let them know myself. I'll be in the office tomorrow if you need me or I'll be by after work to check on y'all."

"Ash?" He turned back, his hand on the doorknob. She wanted him to stay. She didn't want to think about why, but she wanted him by her side, his fingers linked with hers as they faced this threat. She shook her head. "Nothing. Just, be careful."

As the door closed behind him, Jordan wrapped her arms around Levi. She knew without a doubt that she would protect him with a fierceness that she had only imagined up to this point. He rubbed his eyes with a small fist. "I'm sorry, Claire. I'm going to have to take him home and feed him before he falls asleep. I'll see you tomorrow?"

"We'll be here." Claire smiled, but her lips trembled. She was tired. The life she'd chosen was one she wouldn't trade, but Jordan knew that Claire was stretched thin. With Levi in her arms, Jordan walked out the door she had come in, just minutes earlier. Joy and laughter had given way to anxiety.

She nearly bumped into Amelia at the bottom of the steps.

"Okay, Aunt Jordan, the horses are in the pasture with the donkey. Goats are in the barn."

"Goat?" Levi looked hopeful and Jordan laughed.

Amelia grinned. "He said a word!"

"He said *cookie*, too."

Jordan's niece held out her hand for a high five. "Priorities, dude. Welcome to the family. You coming back for dinner?"

"No, I'm headed to the cabin. It's going to be an early night for us."

"Okay, see ya." Amelia bounced up the stairs and slammed open the back door as Jordan circled the pond on the path back to her cottage.

The little trill of nerves was still there in her stomach as she rocked Levi and put him to bed. He was so vulnerable. But it was the warm concern on Ash's face that stuck with her, the undercurrent of anger that simmered under the surface.

She didn't want to need him. Didn't want to need anyone. So why couldn't she get him out of her mind?

Ash dribbled the soccer ball down the field, keeping his eye on the tiny space in the top corner of the goal. He passed forward to his friend Ben Collins just as Joe tackled him, hard. He landed on his butt and bounded back to his feet.

Oh, Joe was asking for it now. Doctors and teachers might be skinnier than Joe and his law enforcement crowd, but muscle didn't mean as much in soccer. He signaled to Ben and put on a burst of speed toward the goal. Ben, always the one to come through in a clutch, sent the ball in a perfect arc to land just in front of Ash's feet.

No hesitation. *Bam.*

He pumped his fist into the air. Game winner. Ben ran forward, shouting, "Goal!" like they did on TV.

Ash's buddy Latham was pointing with both hands at Joe. "Brains before brawn, gentlemen."

Joe laughed. "Next time we're not holding back."

"You do that." Ash snagged a towel and a small bottle of orange juice from the bag he'd left on the hood of his car. They'd been meeting for pickup soccer games since Joe had moved back into town, looking for some exercise that didn't involve weights and a gym. Sometimes the players might change a little bit but for the most part Saturday afternoons meant soccer at the local park.

He pulled his test kit out of the bag, unzipped it, pricking his finger and testing his blood sugar before drinking the juice in one long gulp.

Joe sprawled out on a bench and downed a Gatorade, waving a hand at some of the guys who were leaving. "Your blood sugar okay?"

"Fine. It gets a little low when I exercise but it's not a big deal if I watch it. The monitor will catch it and alert me if it gets into the danger zone."

"It's been a long week," Joe noted.

Latham slung his bag over his shoulder as he walked toward them. "Losers buying dinner?"

"Rain check," Joe said. "I promised Claire I'd get home in time to help get the kids fed and put to bed. It's Mrs. Matthews's day off."

"Lucky you." Ash scrubbed the towel across his sweaty face. "Sorry, Latham, but I've got to go check on a patient after I clean up."

Joe frowned. "Any more kids show up with signs of measles? Claire and Jordan have been driving our kids crazy checking their temperatures."

"Not yet, but it's only been a week. We probably have two more weeks before we're clear. The little girl who came down with it first is out of the hospital, but now her baby brother is in the PICU."

"That's awful. I can't imagine anything worse than one of my kids being sick." Joe stopped, and apparently remembered who he was talking to. "Man, I'm sorry. It does give me perspective on how Mom must have felt when you were sick, though. It was before I came around, but I remember you going every year for your checkup and how happy and relieved Mom was when it was over. She always cooked your favorite foods for dinner that night, remember?"

"I remember." He checked his insulin pump one more time, but it was still firmly in place. He would clean up at home before going to the hospital.

He pulled the strap of his bag over his shoulder and started for his car, Joe falling into step beside him.

"Is there really a chance that any of the kids will get measles? It's not that common, right?"

Ash stopped walking. "Virtually everyone who is exposed to measles and hasn't been vaccinated gets it. The chances are extremely high that other people in town will come down with it, either because they weren't vaccinated or because they needed a booster and didn't get it."

"Well, that's not very reassuring."

"I know. I'm sorry." Ash knew that, in their family, he was the sibling who kept things light. He had health stuff he dealt with on a daily basis. If he couldn't be positive, he couldn't survive.

But this? There wasn't a way to spin a possible measles epidemic. An infectious disease outbreak was one of the things he had nightmares about and he was living it.

* * *

Ash intended to leave the hospital and drive straight home. His body was crying out for some ibuprofen after the brutal soccer game with his brother and their friends. Instead, he drove to Red Hill Farm to check on Levi. He sat in the driveway, the engine of his car ticking quietly.

It was probably too late to go to the door, but the house wasn't dark. He had his hand on the gear shift to put it in Reverse when the door to the cottage opened and light spilled out onto the porch. Gus bolted out the door, stopping to sniff the cool night air before bounding down the trail toward Ash's car.

His decision apparently made for him, he got out and slammed the door behind him. Jordan appeared, silhouetted in the door of the cottage. Ash greeted Gus and gave him a good rub before starting around the pond.

He'd obviously caught her getting ready for bed. Her hair was piled on top of her head, her face freshly scrubbed. Second thoughts once again slowed his steps. "I'm sorry. I'm interrupting. I should go."

"I was about to have some chamomile tea. Want a cup?"

He hesitated again, but honestly, he didn't want to go home and sit in his empty house and worry about them. And yes, he knew he was supposed to give it to God, and he did; it just didn't always seem to stick the way it should.

He sat on the sofa and stared at the flickering candles, which replaced the wood in her fireplace now that it was warmer. She didn't say anything, but he could hear her going through the motions in the kitchen. The bubbling kettle, the clank of ceramic mugs, the hiss as the water met the tea bag.

Something about the ritual calmed the rough edges of his emotions.

Jordan placed the cup on the table beside him and sat on the other end of the couch, her feet curled underneath her.

He sipped the tea—too hot for big gulps.

"Have you heard anything? Anyone new with symptoms?"

"No, it's been really quiet. The incubation period can be up to twenty-one days, though, so I'm not sure we're out of the woods yet. It's way worse than when I imagined something like this in my head. Waiting for the next child to come into the office or for the mom to call and describe the symptoms. It's agonizing."

"I think one of the barn cats is pregnant. I don't know how we ended up with so many cats. We gave all the kittens away except for the one that Joe and Claire kept."

The rapid switch in conversation topic had him blinking, but he realized he didn't want to talk about measles, didn't want to think about measles. "What's the name of the pregnant one?"

"Kat."

His lip twitched. "Very original."

"It's spelled with a K." She met his gaze, unblinking.

He laughed, shaking his head, but he felt about a hundred pounds lighter. First time he'd found anything at all humorous all week. "You're killing me."

"Kat and Gus are best friends." Her big German shepherd was stretched out on a rag rug in front of the fireplace. His tail thumped when he heard his name.

"I make up stories for Levi about the adventures of Kat and Gus."

He took another sip of his tea and relaxed into the pillows of her oversize blue velvet couch.

Being with Jordan was like walking outside after a rainstorm, when the air seemed renewed, cool and fresh. "I want to hear one."

"No! They're only funny if you're three."

"Come on. Last week you said you would owe me a favor when I helped you load in all those bales of hay. I'm calling it."

She laughed and her cheeks pinkened.

"Come on, I'm not leaving until I hear some adventures."

Jordan opened her mouth and his cell phone rang. She grinned.

He muted the ring. "Oh, no. You're not off the hook."

From the bedroom came a little voice. "Mama?"

"Oops, sorry. Gotta check on the munchkin." She popped to her feet and ran for the bedroom door, still laughing, as he answered his phone. "Dr. Sheehan."

"Ash, it's Claire. Sweetness has been crying all afternoon. I just took her temperature. She has a fever of a hundred and two."

"Give her some ibuprofen and try some juice or a Popsicle. I'll come by and check on her in a few minutes. I'm at Jordan's."

He hung up the phone and looked up as Jordan came out of the room with Levi, his little arms around her neck, her face pale.

"What's wrong?"

She lifted her hand. She was holding the ear thermometer and the screen was flashing red. "His temp is a hundred and three."

Chapter Seven

Jordan stood in the door with Levi in her arms. She could feel the heat seeping from his skin to hers. He was so hot. She waited until Ash hung up the phone. "He's burning up."

He was on his feet in a second, looking into Levi's fretful eyes. "Hey, little man, you feeling kind of rough? I bet we can get you feeling better soon. Jordan, where do you keep the children's ibuprofen?"

"It's in the cabinet over the coffeepot, the one with the child lock on it." Her hands were shaking from the adrenaline dumped in her system. She'd reached into the crib to brush the hair from his forehead and his skin was on fire. It was the sign they'd been watching for, waiting for, fearing, these last long few days, but when she reached into that crib, her heart stopped.

Ash was slamming drawers, rummaging around. "You have a syringe?"

"Yes, in the silverware drawer, the one closest to the refrigerator." Levi seemed warmer than he did just minutes ago when she checked his temp. She wondered if she needed to check it again.

"How much does he weigh?"

"Umm, at last check, twenty-two pounds."

Ash frowned, his eyebrows scrunching together under his glasses. "He's still a good bit underweight."

"He weighed seventeen when we left the hospital. He's gotten a lot stronger." In her arms, Levi whimpered and she stroked his little back. "It's okay, buddy. We're getting you some medicine."

Ash shook the bottle and removed the cap. "Okay, the dose is ten milligrams per kilo, twenty-two pounds is right at ten kilos, so a hundred milligrams, or one teaspoon."

"Did you just do that in your head?"

"The math isn't that complicated, plus I do this one every day all day, pretty much." He drew a teaspoon into the syringe and with the ease of lots of practice, squeezed it into Levi's cheek. Miraculously, the three-year-old swallowed instead of spitting it out.

"Impressive," she said. Ash's calm manner and easy competence relieved some of the panic she felt when she'd touched Levi's little head and realized he wasn't just warm.

He grinned. "Nah. I've just had a lot of practice. Have you got a dry-erase pen?"

"Yes, right there on the whiteboard on the refrigerator. Why?"

Those brilliant blue eyes were warm on hers. "A little doctor tip. Use your dry-erase pen and write the time you gave the dose right there on the bottle. Then you know at a glance if you can dose again. And when you do, rub the time off and write it again."

"Good idea for those middle-of-the-night doses. I

do something similar with the horse feed so I remember the ratios I use."

He wrote the time on the bottle and placed it on the counter, the pen next to it. "You can alternate ibuprofen and acetaminophen every three hours to keep his fever from shooting up."

"Thank you, Ash." She rubbed her temple, where she had a shooting pain. "I'm not usually so easily rattled."

His hand slid up her arm to squeeze her shoulder. "It's been a stressful week. I think we're all a little on edge. And fever of one-oh-three is no joke."

She hitched Levi up a little higher and patted him as he coughed. "Who was that on the phone?"

"Claire. Sweetness has a fever, too, so I'm headed over to check on her before I go."

"Oh, no— Do you think— Is there any chance this is just a cold or the flu, maybe?"

He drew in a breath, his eyes serious. "There's always a chance, but we need to be very careful. Don't take Levi out in public and let me know if there are any changes in his condition at all."

"I've never done this before, Ash. What if he's getting worse and I don't know it?" She followed him to the door, where he turned back, standing in the open doorway.

"If we can keep his fever under a hundred and one and he's eating and playing, there's nothing to worry about. If he's lethargic, or if his temp won't come down, call me, no matter what time. Okay?"

She nodded, even though she had tears stinging behind her eyes. "Yes. Ibuprofen and acetaminophen alternating every three hours and call if he gets worse or I can't keep the fever down."

"Exactly." Ash put his arm around her and pulled her close, his rough cheek against her hair. "You'll be fine. I'll see you tomorrow."

He strode out the door and down the stairs toward the farmhouse, where the downstairs lights were still blazing and she could see Claire walking the baby in the kitchen.

Jordan got a juice cup out of the fridge and settled into her favorite chair with Levi in her lap. Levi took a reluctant sip of juice, stuck his thumb in his mouth and stared at her with solemn brown eyes as she rocked gently. "I know you don't feel good, buddy, but you're going to be fine. Dr. Ash is a great doctor and he's going to take good care of you."

The fever reducer kicked in, Levi's little body relaxing. His eyelids began to droop and he slowly drifted to sleep.

She pulled him close, letting his head settle against her chest. This sweet boy had already stolen her heart. She would do anything in her power to protect him, but it really wasn't up to her.

As she rocked, she whispered prayers over him, for healing of his body and healing of his tender spirit, that he would never feel abandoned or unloved or unworthy.

The thought of him being sick with the measles was terrifying, but Ash made her feel like she could handle it. And she knew that he would be there beside them. She'd always been fiercely independent, but with Levi, she was out of her depth. She knew she couldn't do it alone and she was thankful—so thankful—that Ash was by her side in this fight.

* * *

Weak sunlight had just begun to brighten the sky when Ash arrived at Red Hill Farm, and he'd already been to the hospital. The little brother of patient zero was recovering nicely and Ash had given the go-ahead for him to be released this afternoon.

With Claire and Jordan busy with sick babies, Joe was up to his neck getting the other kids out the door. Ash's niece, Amelia, was in charge of feeding the animals, but she usually had Jordan's help, especially in the mornings before school, so Ash had swung by to lend a hand.

As he shoveled fresh wood pellets into one of the stalls, a stall from which he had just removed some very large manure, he wondered just how much he was really helping. One thing was for sure; his Cole Haan loafers would never be the same. "I'm not even sure I'm doing this right."

Amelia glanced his way and shot him a smile. "You are."

She had her hair pulled back in a ponytail with a navy blue ribbon tied at the top to match her school uniform. Her cheeks were pink, skin glowing. Not so much when she'd first come to live with his brother, Joe, but she was beautifully healthy and confident now—an integral part of Red Hill Farm and she knew it.

"Bartlet's the last one. I'll lead him out to the pasture and they can stay out since we canceled lessons this week." A horn sounded and her head jerked up. "Oh, hey, there's my bus. I've gotta run, Uncle Ash."

At the door, she jerked off her boots, grabbed her backpack and ran.

And that left him staring into Bartlet's very large

face. Ash swallowed hard. "Hey—hey Bartlet, you big, um, horse. Good boy."

Tentatively, he stroked the horse's neck and was rewarded with horse spit blown in his face. "Yeah, good boy. Okay, I know we're not really friends, but your, um, Jordan is busy with Levi, and Amelia had to go to school, so here we are."

A month ago he would not have believed that he would be in the barn trying to be friendly with a horse. A very big horse. And yet, here he was.

Jordan pushed him to be a better, stronger person. Bartlet was just a horse, but somehow this change seemed much bigger than that. He'd been going through the motions in his life. Work, home, repeat. Sure there had been women, social events, but no one that made him feel...anything.

Jordan had been different from the jump. "She's passionate about everything. Even you. Especially you and the kids you help."

The more he scratched and rubbed the giant head, the more at ease he felt. However, rubbing and scratching wasn't going to get Bartlet into the pasture.

A bright yellow lead was on a nail next to Bartlet's stall. Ash looped the rope in one hand, then tried to sneak the hook onto Bartlet's...bridle? Halter? He had no idea which, but either way, Bartlet wasn't having it.

The horse shook his mane and bobbed his head, which was three times the size of Ash's. Ash backed up a step. "Okay, dude. You may be able to crush me under your feet, but it's my job to get you to the grass. You like grass, right?"

Bartlet rolled his eyes.

"Sure, you do, big fella." Ash made his voice as

soothing as possible, like he did with kids who were afraid of the doctor. "You like grass and that's where we're going."

This time when he tried to connect the lead rope, he made contact. *Yes.*

He unhooked the latch on the barn door, eased it open and clicked his tongue. Bartlet walked out like a big old Southern gentleman. Ash held his breath until he got him into the pasture, especially when the other horses and the donkey felt the need to run full speed straight at him, wheeling to a stop to greet Bartlet.

A deep breath and a couple of big steps and his back met the pasture fence. He ducked under and stepped over, straightened and saw Jordan watching from the other side of the ring where they did therapy sessions, a goofy smile on her tired face.

She had on a turquoise denim ball cap with a faded red patch. Her braids had been traded for a low pony-tail. He could only guess she hadn't had time to mess with the braids.

He walked closer and couldn't quite stifle the proud-of-himself smile. "Levi okay?"

"Mrs. Matthews had measles when she was a little girl so she stopped by with some cookies and told me to take a nap, but animals come before napping, so I thought I'd take a look and see how far Amelia got this morning. I can't believe you did this." Her eyes filled and the words came out half-sob half-laugh. "Your shoes are all messed up."

He ducked under and stepped through again and, on her side of the fence, he wrapped his arms around her. "You're so beautiful."

She snorted a laugh into his shoulder. "You've lost your mind. I'm exhausted."

"But you're exhausted because you love that little guy and you've been there when he needed you. That is beautiful to me." Ash knew he'd been drawn here from the first time he saw her. Maybe he'd fought too hard, or maybe he hadn't fought hard enough, but in this moment, all of his reasons not to reach for her just disappeared.

He cupped her face in his hands, tilted it up and gently kissed her lips and weepy eyes. He pulled her close again, holding her there against his chest, letting go of the need to control every single situation and letting himself just...feel.

A horse nickered from the other side of the fence. Jordan stepped back, scrubbing the tears off her face. She sent Ash a trembling smile as she walked toward the fence, leaving him standing there wondering what happened to his heart...and his resolve.

The horses and donkey crowded the fence and, one by one, she fed them carrots from her pocket. The goats got wind that food was happening and gathered around her feet, and he smiled because they made her laugh with their silly antics. They definitely weren't as polite as the horses, but she fed them carrots, too.

When she ran out, she held up her empty hands and the animals scattered. "Mooches."

Ash grabbed his medical bag from the car and fell into step beside her as she walked back to the cottage. "Where's Gus?"

She glanced up and in the gray, damp day, her eyes glowed blue-green. "Inside. Levi's cough is worse and Gus refuses to leave him."

On the porch steps, he stomped the mud and who knows what else off his shoes. "Let me get out of these and I'll be right in to take a look at him."

She went through the door into her small cottage and he stared at the bright coral door that she closed behind her. Like the colors she surrounded herself with, Jordan was a bright spot.

The moment by the barn may have been a long time coming but he knew it changed things. And he had to decide if he could overcome the fear—yes, he could name it that—he had about relationships.

Jordan wasn't the person to have a casual relationship with, and if he wanted to be a part of her life, he was going to have to make some fundamental changes in his.

Jordan picked Levi up from the high chair, where he hadn't touched his food. "Not hungry, little man?"

Levi coughed, the sound wet and thick. Gus nudged his foot and his big black tail wagged.

"I'm worried about that cough." Mrs. Matthews picked up the plate from the table and rinsed it. "He seems to be getting worse."

Kissing his forehead, Jordan frowned at how warm it was. She'd just given him ibuprofen an hour ago and he still seemed feverish. "Ash is coming in to check on Levi as soon as he gets his feet clean enough. He was mucking the stall in loafers."

The door opened behind her. "I heard that."

His bold blue eyes were laughing when she turned around. She raised an eyebrow. "Well, I mean, if you're such a greenhorn that you wear loafers to work in the barn, you have to expect us to poke a little fun."

In his sock feet, he walked closer and placed his bag on the counter, reaching behind him to turn the light on. Levi winced and Ash leaned closer to take a look in his eyes. "No matting there yet, but the sensitivity to light is a symptom."

Levi buried his head in Jordan's shoulder. Ash rubbed the stethoscope between his hands to warm it and slid it under the little T-shirt. Jordan was so close to him, she could feel his breath. He was listening, small lines of concentration forming on his forehead.

Maybe it was silly, but he was caring for her baby and that made him even more attractive than he was before. She wouldn't have said that would be possible, but somehow, it was.

A thick golden lock fell to curl on his forehead. Her fingers itched to smooth it.

He stepped back. "I'm a little concerned about the cough. It's not terrible right now, but we have no way of knowing how much his lungs were affected by the environment he was living in before foster care. I think I'm going to call in an antibiotic for him. It won't help the measles but it might help with the complications."

"You think he has the measles for sure?" Loads of people, like Mrs. Matthews, had the measles as a child and survived it. Jordan didn't know why the idea scared her so much. Maybe because Levi was still fragile. She didn't know if he had the strength to fight off a virus like this.

"His symptoms are consistent." Ash's hands were gentle on Levi's head as he took a look in the little boy's ears. "We'll know for sure if the rash pops up in the next day or so. Hey, buddy, can you open your mouth?"

Levi obediently opened his mouth, which reminded

Jordan again that he understood so much more than he communicated.

That little furrow between Ash's brows reappeared.

"What?" Jordan didn't like that look.

"Can you see those tiny white spots?"

She turned Levi around and laid him back in her arms. He squirmed but didn't cry.

Ash pointed the small light into the toddler's mouth. Little grayish-white spots populated the inside of his cheeks. "Measles?"

"They're called Koplik spots and they're the hallmark of measles. He'll break out in the rash in the next day or two. I'm sorry, Jordan. I know you were hoping it was anything else but this."

Tears hovered close to the surface. "I don't know if he's strong enough to fight it off."

He put his arm around the two of them and bent his head to nearly touch hers.

Mrs. Matthews busied herself quickly at the kitchen sink.

"We're going to take care of him, Jordan. I promise, we will." Ash put his stethoscope and otoscope back in place in his medical bag. "I'm going to check on Claire before I head to the office." He looked down at his sock feet and muddy khakis. "Mmm, maybe I'll run by the house before I go in."

Jordan laughed shakily. "That might be a good idea. I mean, I find essence of horse irresistible, but it might be a little off-putting for some of your patients."

"Irresistible?" Ash widened his eyes and made a silly grab for her, which she easily skirted. "Taking note."

He was still laughing as he closed the door behind

him. Jordan handed Levi to Mrs. Matthews and opened the door. Ash was sitting on the steps, pulling on his disgusting loafers. "Yeah, I think these might be toast."

It wasn't that he was handsome, even though he was. It wasn't even that he was nice to everyone, though he was that, too. It was that heart of his, that part of him that she'd missed when all she'd seen was what he showed the world. That was what drew her to him now. He'd ruined his shoes because he came over to help Amelia feed the horses, even though he was afraid of them.

"Thank you, Ash." She didn't know what else to say, really. The feelings were too big.

He nodded. "Anytime."

She went back into the cottage. Mrs. Matthews, in the rocking chair with Levi, gave her a knowing look. She patted Levi, who was nearly asleep on her considerable chest. "Children are not ours, you know, Jordan. They're God's. He loved them before we even knew they would be in existence. He's got Levi right in the palm of His hand."

Jordan nodded, not trusting herself to say anything without the dam breaking and sobs rushing out. God loved Levi before he was born, loved him when he was still with his biological parents and loved him now.

Even through the measles.

Maybe this wasn't what she would choose for Levi. Maybe she didn't understand why it happened when Levi had been through so much, but she had to trust in God's plan.

She needed Him.

And in her dim bedroom, as she climbed in between

the cool sheets and began to drift, the thought wouldn't leave her mind that she knew she needed the Lord, but maybe she needed Ash Sheehan a little bit, too.

Chapter Eight

A towel draped around his neck, Ash leaned on his car and dug his phone out of his gym bag. "Same time Saturday?"

His brother grinned and pulled out his own phone. "If you're really sure you want to get beat again. Oh, man. Claire's called me seven times."

Ash looked at the face of his phone and all frivolity vanished. He had ten missed calls from Jordan. Only an emergency would warrant that kind of determination. Ash's phone buzzed in his hand and he slid his finger across the surface of the screen. "Jordan?"

"Ash!" The word came through noise that sounded like she was standing in a hurricane.

"Where are you? What's going on?"

"Levi's being life-flighted to the hospital. He couldn't keep anything down and then he had a seizure and I couldn't wake him up. Can you meet us there?"

"I'm on my way. Praying."

There was no response. The call just ended.

This wasn't Ash's first patient to be life-flighted, but Levi wasn't just any patient. He stood there a second, staring at the phone, unfamiliar nerves jangling. Joe was pacing, his phone still glued to his ear.

Joe hung up. "Man, I'm sorry. Claire and I want to go to the hospital but she can't leave the baby and I need to get home to give Mrs. Matthews a break from the other kids."

"I don't know for sure, but he'll probably be kept in the PICU tonight so you'd just be sitting in the waiting room, anyway. I'll keep you updated." Ash opened the back door of his Lexus and tossed his exercise bag into the back seat.

"We'll be praying." Joe was still standing there when Ash slammed the car door shut and drove away.

With privileges at the hospital, he went straight there. He searched the ER for the two of them. As usual, the department was chaos, albeit carefully orchestrated chaos. He found Jordan leaning on the wall outside one of the isolation rooms, her face in her hands.

"Jordan?"

She looked up and her eyes filled. He opened his arms and she walked into them. "I'm so scared."

"I know." He was shaken with the need to take away the fear and worry, to take her pain onto his shoulders.

"I don't know what's going on. They've been working on him since we got here and they won't let me be with him."

"They'll be out soon." He laced his fingers with hers and leaned his back against the wall beside her. "I'll wait with you. You said he had a seizure?"

She nodded. "For most of the day he seemed, well, not fine but okay. Then he started throwing up and his eyes just rolled back in his head."

The door to the isolation room opened and a couple of nurses came out, pulling off their masks and paper gowns. Ash couldn't tell from their faces what was going on. Anxiety rose like acid in his throat.

He knew all the things that could go wrong in the body, what kind of ravages infection could leave. It was why he worked tirelessly to sharpen the skills he needed to fight them. He stabbed his fingers into his hair.

Why Levi? That little guy had been through so much already.

The door opened again and a man in dark blue scrubs stepped out and, after shedding his mask and gown, stuck his hand under the dispenser for the bactericidal gel. A pediatric intensivist and infectious disease specialist Ash knew well, the ED had apparently called him down for a consult. "James. How is he?"

Dr. McIntyre turned, his eyes brightening when he saw Ash. "Ash, good to see you. This patient's one of yours? His oh-two sat was eighty-six when he came in. Portable CT detected pneumonia—left lung was practically a whiteout."

"Would you mind using layman's terms? This is his foster mom, Jordan."

"Sorry. Levi was conscious when he arrived but his oxygen level was very low. The infection in the lungs is making it hard for him to breathe. Dr. Sheehan can weigh in here, but the plan will be to treat the measles with IVIG, the pneumonia with antibiotics. Because of the seizure and his general grogginess, we did a head CT, which was negative. We'll do another one tomorrow to make sure that the seizure was induced by the rapid rise of fever and not encephalitis."

It was a lot for a new mom to take in. Ash put his arm around Jordan's shoulders. She trembled with tension, like a guitar string about to break.

James glanced at the clock at the end of the hall and back at Jordan. "The next twenty-four hours are critical, but we're going to do everything we can. He's sedated so he won't fight the machine helping him breathe, so if you want to go ho—"

"I'm not leaving him." The tone of her voice left no room for questions.

A nurse stuck her head out of one of the exam rooms. "Dr. McIntyre, can I grab you for a second?"

James smiled at Jordan, but his eyes were kind as he backed toward the room and his next patient. "I figured you'd want to stay. We're taking him up to the PICU in a few minutes. You can wait in the waiting area for family members until he's settled."

"This way." Jordan's hand in his, Ash walked toward the elevator. She didn't speak and he didn't know what to say. He was used to comforting parents of sick children, but this wasn't just any parent of any sick child. This was Jordan.

His own heart was constricted into a barely beating mass because worry for a child he'd grown to love consumed him. He—of all people—knew how fickle life could be. Doctors did their best, but sometimes there just was no explanation why things went the way they did.

The PICU waiting room held a handful of other people, some reading, some sleeping, one staring at a television that no one could hear.

Ash sat for about ten seconds before he was up and pacing the small room. His phone buzzed in his hand, his glucose monitor reminding him he hadn't eaten anything after his workout with the guys.

He grabbed a cookie and poured two cups of stale coffee, taking one to Jordan, who couldn't sit, either. She was staring out the window at the air-conditioning units on the roof of the second floor, but he didn't think she was seeing them. "We're gonna get him through this, J."

"I know." She took a sip of the coffee, made a face and took another sip as the loudspeaker crackled to life.

"Code blue. PICU. Code blue. PICU."

The cup of coffee slid from Jordan's fingers, hitting the terrazzo floor and splattering everywhere. She grabbed napkins from the table and dropped to her knees, trying to wipe the soppy mess, the words *code blue* reverberating in her head. *Code blue. Code blue. Code blue.*

She folded, her head on her knees, unable to breathe. Ash's arms came around her, lifting her to her feet and guiding her to a chair.

One of the other mothers got up and without a word cleaned up the mess, a different person pouring another cup of coffee and handing it to Jordan.

A nurse appeared in the door. "Thomas family?"

Silent tears slid down the cheeks of the mother who had poured the coffee for Jordan. Her husband grabbed her hand and they walked into the hall for a short, tense conversation with the nurse before disappearing down the hall.

The grief and fear in the room was palpable. These people wouldn't be in this waiting area unless they were with someone in pediatric ICU and, if their children were in this unit, those young lives were in peril.

Maybe it wasn't her child who coded this time, but it could have been. The code was for someone's child, a someone who loved that child as much as she loved Levi—as much as these other parents loved their children.

Please keep him safe. Please, Lord, please keep him safe. There were no elaborate prayers, no fancy words or church language that could make this better, only the presence of the Lord, who knew Levi, had known him from the beginning.

Please keep him safe, Lord. Please.

Ash's fingers squeezed hers, silent reassurance.

Dr. McIntyre stepped into the open door. He didn't even have to say her name before she was on her feet and out in the hall. "How is he?"

"We've got him in the isolation room and he's stable, so you can go see him. You can stay with him if you want. Parents are allowed twenty-four-hour access." Dr. McIntyre put his hand on Ash's arm. "Dr. Sheehan, can I see you a minute?"

"I'll be right there, Jordan."

She hesitated, but pushed the button for the double doors and walked through them to the nurses' station. "I'm looking for Levi Wheeler?"

The nurse closest to her looked up. "Your wristband, please?"

Jordan showed the wristband she'd been given in the ED, which had her identification and Levi's.

The nurse scanned it. "You're his mother?"

"Foster mom. I'm authorized to be with him and to sign for his medical care."

The nurse handed her ID back and rounded the counter. "I'm Brenda. I'm the charge nurse. Our unit has a one-to-one nurse-patient ratio and doctors are on the unit at all times. Because Levi has the measles, we have some precautions in place that we'll have to follow."

Brenda helped Jordan get a gown and shoe protectors and then said, "If you're immune to measles, respiratory protection is optional."

The wall and door into Levi's room were glass. Jordan's eyes fixed on the tiny little guy in the bed. He wasn't moving. "I've been vaccinated."

"Okay. Every time you go in, you gown up and use the bactericidal gel. When you come out, you toss the gown and use the gel again before leaving the unit. Got it?"

Jordan nodded and used some of the sanitizer before entering the room. There was a nurse in the room with Levi, typing on a rolling monitoring station, but Jordan barely glanced at her.

Levi had wires and pads attached in all different places, some labeled with letters. He had IVs, a couple of them, and there were monitors everywhere.

She didn't realize she was walking until she stood at his bedside, her hand reaching for Levi, but there was no place for her to touch him. Finally, she ran her finger down the soft skin of his hand. "Hey, buddy, I'm here with you."

The nurse, super skinny with a frizz of gray curls, walked to the bedside. Like the other nurse, she wore turquoise scrubs and a bright long-sleeved shirt underneath the pale yellow paper gown. "I'm Erin and I'm taking care of Levi overnight. The wires and tubes look scary but they're in place to either help Levi or help us monitor his condition."

The door whooshed open behind her. Ash stepped into the room. He, too, had a gown and foot protectors on. He stepped into place beside Jordan, his arm sliding protectively around her. "Hey, Erin. How's the little man doing?"

"Dr. Sheehan." Erin's voice was warm with welcome. "Always good to see you. Levi's vitals improved once we got him settled. The BiPAP is working to keep his sats up. Dr. McIntyre is hopeful we can avoid the vent."

"That's good news. Thanks." He showed Jordan the bags hanging from the pole. "One of those is antibiotics to fight off the pneumonia. This one is IVIG to help his immune system fight off the measles."

Jordan nodded. She didn't trust her voice. This little guy was depending on her and she was so out of her league.

The nurse, Erin, stepped out.

Ash pointed to two little red lights, one wrapped around Levi's fingertip and one on his big toe. "Those are pulse oximeters. They tell us his oxygen level. That mask he has over his nose helps air get into his lungs, but if his oxygen saturation drops below 90 again, they'll intubate him."

"Is that blood? Why is he getting that?"

"Extra red blood cells make it easier for his blood to carry oxygen to his whole body."

Jordan walked to the door, looked out at nothing and paced back again, nerves making her edgy, restless. "I know I should be relieved that he's here and he's stable, but instead I'm mad. This is too much. I don't want him to be in the hospital again. He was just beginning to trust me."

"He's not going to lose that trust, Jordan. He loves you and he's going to depend on you while he's here to be his safe place."

"You think so?" She desperately wanted it to be true. They had both worked so hard the past few weeks to overcome the trauma that Levi experienced and begin to bond.

"Yes, I do. He needs you." He pulled her closer into the circle of his arm and she leaned in.

He was so calm and she just was...not. "Thank you for being here with us, Ash."

"Where else would I be?"

She looked at her phone. It was almost one in the morning. "I don't know. Asleep? You have patients tomorrow."

"I'll grab a nap in the on-call room later, no big deal. Why don't you sit down in that recliner for a bit while I'm here to keep an eye on Levi?"

Jordan sat down. She'd been up for days with a very sick toddler, but she couldn't relax. Her mind knew there was nothing left for her to do, but her body hadn't caught up with her mind, apparently.

"Close your eyes. I'll be right here."

Just that one statement seemed to still the panicked beating of her heart. She knew she could take Ash at his word. Through heavy-lidded eyes, she watched him as he checked Levi's IVs with gentle fingers, and nearly came undone as he brushed a kiss across the small forehead.

Ash texted something on his phone and a couple of minutes later someone came to the door and passed in a blanket. He tucked the blanket, fresh from the warmer, around her, and then her eyes wouldn't stay open.

As her mind drifted, she realized that she wasn't afraid anymore. Ash was there and he would take care of them both.

Sometimes being a doctor was awesome. He had patients who had such faith in him that every time they had a skinned knee they wanted to come to his office for him to make it better. Days like today—when his waiting room filled with parents anxious about a measles outbreak—put his parent-reassurance skills—and frankly, his patience—to the test.

He'd spent most of the day wishing he was at the hospital with Jordan and had come as quickly as possible after his last patient left. He scanned his ID card to get into the PICU. Jordan had texted him every couple of hours to give him an update, but it wasn't the same as having his eyes on Levi.

The door opened and Levi's doctor was standing on the other side. "Ash. I was hoping I would catch you. Levi Wheeler—I know you have a personal interest. He's not turning the corner like I hoped he would. He's stable, just not better."

"Do you think the antibiotic has the right coverage?"

"I'm not sure. I added a different one this afternoon. We were planning to lighten his sedation today but I think we're going to give him another night on the BiPAP."

Ash closed his eyes and rubbed his fingers over the spot in the middle of his forehead that hurt. His eyes popped open. "He was neglected. We don't usually think of Vitamin A for kids over two years old, but Levi was suffering from malnutrition and failure to thrive. There's a good chance he's deficient. If he is, it could help."

McIntyre smiled. "I should've thought of that. I'll put the order in."

"Measles, we're comin' for ya." Ash grinned and pushed off the wall. "I'm going to check on Levi now."

From outside the door he could see Jordan standing by Levi's bed, reading him a story. He put the gown and shoes on and stuck his hand under the automatic dispenser for the bactericidal gel and entered the room where two of his favorite people were.

His step hitched.

Two of his favorite people. When did that happen?

Jordan glanced up from the book, her blue-green eyes looking a little tired. "He's still sedated, but I thought maybe the sound of my voice would be sooth-ing."

"I'm sure it is." He walked a little closer. Jordan's cheeks were flushed. "You feeling okay?"

"Tired."

Ash put his hand on her forehead and she swatted him away. "I'm fine."

"Jordan. Your eyes are red. Your cheeks are flushed."

"I'm not sick." She turned on her heel and wavered, reaching a hand out for the rail of Levi's bed. "I'm not."

He reached for her forehead again and this time she let him. She was burning up. "You need to be in bed."

"I'm not leaving Levi. I'm not…leaving…" Her eyes fluttered closed and she started to fall.

Ash caught her midway to the cold hospital floor and eased her into the reclining chair. He slammed the call button by Levi's bed. "Can I get some help in here, please?"

He brushed damp hair away from Jordan's face. "You stubborn, stubborn woman. You just...need to get well. Okay, Jordan? Just get well."

Chapter Nine

Jordan opened her eyes and, as light speared in, closed them again immediately. Ouch. The last thing she remembered was being mad at Ash for saying that she was sick, when clearly she was just tired from being up with Levi for the past few days.

Levi.

Putting her hand on her aching head, she narrowed her eyes into slits to keep the light from making it worse. She turned her head toward the window and saw the most beautiful sight. Levi was in the crib next to her bed. No more PICU, no more BiPAP. He had a very thin tube for oxygen around his face, and all but one of the IVs were gone. He was sitting up, playing with two brightly colored monster trucks.

Beside him, dozing in what looked like the most uncomfortable chair ever made, was Ash. She'd obviously been out for a while and he'd picked up her slack, making sure Levi had the care he needed. What kind of person was she that she had thought him selfish and shallow?

In his every action, he had shown that he wasn't. He

was steadfast. Unfortunately, that fact didn't change anything. Not really. He was still the handsome doctor with a different girl on his arm each week. And she was still the same person she'd always been, an introverted farm girl who was more comfortable with horses than people.

She wanted to call out to them, but her eyes were so achy and tired. Maybe if she closed them for a minute…

The next time Jordan woke, the room was in shadows. The sun had gone down. She wasn't even sure it was the same day. Turning her head, she took stock.

A small overnight bag was next to a small vase of flowers on the windowsill. Her sister had been here. Or more likely Mrs. Matthews.

Levi was asleep in the crib next to her, a soft blue blanket pulled to his shoulders and a stuffed elephant clutched in his arms. The nasal cannula was still in place but he was looking more like himself, with most of the wires and tubes gone.

When she sat up in bed, Ash looked up from his phone with a smile. "Hey, you're awake."

"Hey." She was awake, alive and wishing a little desperately for a hairbrush and a toothbrush. She settled instead for a sip of some lukewarm water that was sitting at her bedside.

"Levi's doing great. His fever stayed around a hundred today and he went a couple of hours without oxygen this afternoon, so they're hoping he'll be able to wean off the cannula tomorrow."

"I guess I have the measles?"

"You guess right, but your case isn't as severe as Levi's, probably because you were vaccinated as a child. I'm hoping both of you guys will be sleeping in your own bed by tomorrow night." He moved and she realized that the IV pole, which she thought was just in the room, was attached to his arm.

Alarmed, she swung her feet over the edge of the bed. "Ash, what's going on? Are you sick?"

He glanced at the IV in his arm and made a face. "No, just getting some fluids and electrolytes."

"Why do you need to do that?"

"You remember me telling you about having cancer as a kid?" When she nodded, he went on. "I had chemo and radiation, too, which killed the cancer in my kidneys but also radiated part of my pancreas. I've had insulin-dependent diabetes since I was seven years old."

He lifted his shirt and showed her a couple of box-like things attached to his belly. "This one's an insulin pump and this one is a glucose monitor. They work together and make the kind of diabetes I have more manageable. Um, sorry. I hope that doesn't gross you out."

"It's not gross—they help keep you alive. Why didn't you tell me?" Her heart ached for him. He'd been such a little boy to deal with something so life-altering.

"It's been a part of me for so long that monitoring my glucose levels and adjusting insulin is just a part of the day-to-day, kind of like...did you know that I drink a green smoothie every day for breakfast?"

"I did not. Like, with spinach?" She made a face.

"Kale."

"Ooh, hard-core. I guess you don't put ice cream in yours, huh?"

He cut his eyes at her. "I do not. Put ice cream. In my green smoothie."

"So why do you need an IV?"

His eyes flickered to hers at the abrupt subject change. "Because when I'm exhausted or dehydrated, and I'm both, my body gets out of whack. I'm sorry."

"What? Why? I'm sorry!"

Frowning at her, he dragged his IV pole over to her and sat on the end of her bed. "Why are you sorry?"

"I got sick and left you to deal with Levi all on your own. And you obviously haven't left his side."

"I look that bad, huh?" His smile was quick and rueful as he rubbed the stubble on his chin.

As if. It seemed impossible, but he was even more handsome with the scruff. She raised an eyebrow. "Pretty bad."

Ash chuckled. "In that case, I need a favor."

"Anything."

"Really? Anything? You don't want to know what it is first?"

She narrowed her eyes. "Now you're scaring me. What is it?"

"I have to go to this fund-raiser in a couple of weeks, one that's important to me. I need a date."

She hesitated.

"You did say anything, remember."

"Can I wear my boots?"

"No." He smiled and her heart forgot to beat for a second. He was exhausted and stubbly and still his smile could make her swoon.

"Okay."

"Okay? Really?" There was genuine surprise and excitement in his voice.

She was already regretting this decision. But she

did owe him one and if that was what he wanted…
"I think you know what you're getting into with me
by now, so if my being your date is you calling in the
favor, you got it."

"I'll text you the details when I'm awake enough to
remember them."

Levi stirred and whimpered in his crib. Jordan stood
up, swayed and sat back down to regroup.

She tried again and this time she made it to the sweet
boy's bed, only coughing a little bit. She smoothed his
hair away from his forehead and sang again the song
she had sung to him the first time she saw him and almost every day since—*Our God is a great big God
and He holds us in His hand.*

The little boy relaxed and he curled up around his
stuffed animal, tucking his hands under his chin as
she stroked his soft curls. She covered him with the
fuzzy fleece blanket, her legs shaking with the effort
of standing so long.

When she turned around, Ash was sound asleep on
her bed, legs curled up, feet hanging off the bed. She
drew the blanket over his shoulders and stood there a
moment, taking in his beautiful face, even with three
days of stubble, even with lines carved from exhaus-
tion. Those small imperfections only made him more
attractive, given the reason behind them.

She resisted the urge to smooth his hair like she had
Levi's. He had many more layers to him than she'd first
thought. He was still that guy—the easygoing, guitar-
playing ladies' man—but the more she was around
him, the more she realized he wasn't *just* that guy. He
was real and deep and…complicated.

She got another blanket out of the closet in the room

and settled into the reclining chair to let Ash get a few hours of sleep.

He'd stepped up and been her rock through this whole experience. Tomorrow they were checking out. And as much as she wanted to be at home in her own bed, there was a part of her that would miss having him right by her side. Things wouldn't be the same after they left the hospital, and they shouldn't be.

She didn't want to need him. But somehow, despite her best effort, she did.

Jordan sat at her computer, a huge mug of coffee at her fingertips. She and Levi had been home for four days, but his schedule was all out of whack. Consequently, she was severely sleep-deprived and, if she was being honest, still a little weak from being so sick.

Her spreadsheet was open on the monitor and crunching numbers was giving her a headache. She'd moved here with six horses and a financial cushion, not a large one, but still. How she'd managed to go through that amount of money was beyond her, except that she could see it in black-and-white on the screen. It was horse feed and medicine, fence repair, tack repair, equipment, building maintenance.

Horses were expensive.

She'd also been sidetracked by a certain little tyke with big brown eyes and a mop of curly hair. That and a case of the measles no one could have predicted.

She was exhausted.

But then she looked at her bulletin board, where she'd tacked pictures of each of her clients. Each of them had a diagnosis and a treatment plan, but they weren't their diagnoses. They were Juliet and Evan and

Portia and Elizabeth Ann and, well, each one of them had a name. Each of them deserved her best.

A quick knock had her looking up to greet her volunteer coordinator, Allison, a tiny powerhouse with a flippy blond ponytail and a tennis skirt. "Hey, coffee's on. Grab a cup and we'll talk about what's coming up."

Allison's husband had developed an app that made him a kajillionaire before the age of thirty, so she decided to leave her job as an event planner at a major hotel and take her many talents to a job she enjoyed. Jordan thanked God every day that she'd answered the phone when Allison called looking for a nonprofit to plug into. The woman knew everyone in a sixty mile radius and had a knack of making them think volunteering was their own idea.

She dragged a chair up to Jordan's desk, which now occupied a corner of the living area, and pulled her tablet out of a giant Louis Vuitton bag. "Okay, I sent you the volunteer schedule for this week. Unless we add new clients to the schedule, we're covered for all of our therapy appointments. I have people lined up to exercise all of the horses except for Freckles and I have Amelia on him."

Jordan made a notation on her to-do list—which she kept on a pad of paper. "Great. Send me the schedules and I'll post them on the big board in the barn."

Allison swiped and tapped. "Done. Next order of business. I've had parents asking about adding speech therapy again. I wondered what you thought about me putting out some feelers to see if we could get someone, maybe one day a week for starters until we see how much interest there is."

Jordan did the occupational therapy and more recently, she had added a physical therapist two days a week. Hippotherapy was integrated therapy and many of their kids had multifaceted needs.

A speech therapist could add another layer to the care they were able to provide. It was a good idea. "Let's start with one day a week to work with clients and request that he or she be present at planning meetings."

"Got it. I have someone in mind, so I'll talk to her and see if I can get her on board." Allison made another notation in her tablet and looked up. "That's all I wanted to talk about. Anything else we need to discuss?"

"When you came in, I was sitting here trying to figure out what we could do to generate some revenue. I have a couple ideas."

Allison's hazel eyes were curious. "Come on, lemme hear 'em."

"First…birthday parties. We don't have therapy sessions on Saturday, so we could book parties on Saturday afternoons. Having just two or three themes might make it easier." She paused, thinking. "Maybe Royal Birthday and Cowboy Birthday."

"Saddle up for a Rip-Roaring Good Time." Allison's fingers were flying on her tablet, but she looked up with a grin.

Jordan blinked. "Whatever you say."

"We need a couple more picnic tables and until we get our covered arena, we'd have to give rain checks for rainy days, but it's definitely doable!"

"Your mind works at the speed of light. I like it."

"You're the one who thought of it!" Allison's ponytail bobbed enthusiastically. She started typing again.

"I think I have a volunteer with just the skills and connections to pull this off. I just sent her an email, so I'll let you know."

"Perfect. The other idea is beginning horseback riding lessons when we have openings in the schedule. We could do group lessons or private. Since we're still building our client base, it could be a way to increase revenue."

"You would teach?"

"Yeah. Or Claire. She's as qualified as I am to teach lessons, maybe more so. She used to compete. I'll talk to her about it."

"Sounds good to me. I have some time this week so I'll make up a flyer and send it to you for your approval."

"Allison." Jordan waited until her friend and assistant looked up. "I seriously love you."

Allison giggled, her laugh as infectious and bubbly as the rest of her personality. "I love you, too. I'm gonna get out of here before I volunteer for another job."

"Shoot me an email if you have any questions."

Allison tucked her tablet back into her ginormous purse and started for the door. "Where's my sweet buddy today?"

"He's with Mrs. Matthews. We're trying to get back into a normal rhythm."

"I'm glad you're feeling better. That was so scary, although I understand the very handsome Dr. Sheehan never left your side."

Heat blasted Jordan's cheeks. "I don't know that I would say it exactly like that. We're friends and he's Levi's doctor."

"Whatever you say. But next time, if you're going to be hanging out with the hot doc, I'd like to know before I hear it from the prayer chain."

Jordan laughed. "Of course. I don't know what I was thinking. I'll see you later."

The whirlwind of efficiency that was Allison was out the door as fast as she had come in. Jordan looked at the spreadsheet again, but now that they had concrete plans in motion for generating more operating funds, she didn't feel quite so panicky.

Now they just needed time…and a covered arena.

She dug through the notepads on her desk until she found the one marked Prayer List and flipped to the page with current prayer requests. Under the line that said, *Karli adjusts to her new orthosis*, she wrote, *Covered Arena*.

Under that one, and she wasn't even sure why, she wrote, *Ash*.

Ash stepped out of the kitchen and onto the back porch at Red Hill Farm. Claire's foster daughter Sweetness was healing up nicely from the measles. Her case hadn't been quite as severe as Levi's but her symptoms had stretched out a little longer.

The place was looking good. Claire had shared with him that some of their neighbors had put a sign-up sheet in the Hilltop Café so that people could volunteer to help out around the farm while the kids were sick. One grandpa even helped the older kids with their homework so that Claire could focus on Sweetness, and he liked it so much that he was going to come back every week to tutor.

Ash understood. These kids—and their foster parents—had a way of getting under your skin.

Jordan was in the ring with a client. Ash took the steps down and crossed the yard, intending to watch from the rails, and then realized the little boy on the small horse was Levi. Jordan looked up at Levi, her lips moving. The three-year-old smiled and waved at Ash.

Something in his eye pricked suspiciously like tears but he blinked them back. Levi had come so far from the terrified child they had found at the hospital the first night. Like Jordan, Ash had worried a little that a new hospital stay would set the toddler back, but instead it seemed to have cemented the bond among them all.

Jordan let Levi slide off the horse and into her arms. The volunteer working with her tied Hagrid off at the post where they did the grooming.

Ash leaned his elbows on the fence. "I need to talk to you."

"That sounds ominous." She walked closer to the fence.

Before he could speak again, Kiera, one of their teenagers, called out. "Hey, Aunt J, Mrs. Matthews is letting us decorate some cookies. We want Levi to come and help."

"Of course. Want cookies, Levi?"

He grinned and patted her cheek. "Cookie."

"Guess that's a yes." She passed him over the fence into Kiera's arms. "I'll be over in a little while to get him."

Ash watched the teenager, who had a baby of her own, bounce toward the house with a giggling Levi. "They're giving him a family."

"Yes, they are." Jordan grinned. "I'm glad you can see that. It was one of the things that Claire and I wanted so badly—for the kids who came to live here to know they were wanted and loved and part of something. They're not just a paycheck and this is not just a way station. It's a real home."

"There's no question you've achieved that."

Jordan disappeared into the barn and came out the door with a couple of canned drinks. "Join me on the swing?"

They settled into the swing, which was attached to a branch of a giant oak tree. He cracked open his drink and took a swig. "So have you thought about making it permanent with Levi?"

"Permanent…family, you mean?"

"Yes. Adoption."

She didn't answer, just stared into the distance, where a couple of the kids, the twins probably, had found a mud puddle and were taking turns jumping in it.

"I didn't mean to upset you. You don't have to answer that."

"I don't think about it. It would be easy to, because he doesn't visit with any family, but I don't." She shook her head and her eyes filled, even though a small smile lifted the corners of her lips. "That's not true. It's what I want to be true. I want to be a team player, but I think about it all the time, mainly because he is getting attached and the idea of putting him through another separation and adjustment, or worse, putting him in a dangerous situation, nearly kills me."

He linked their fingers. "You're stunning, you know."

"What? *No.*"

"You're willing to sacrifice your own peace of mind

so that Levi can know what a real home, a real mother, is like." That bravery and strength Jordan exuded wasn't an act; it was a part of her, one he admired so much.

"It's not a sacrifice. Getting to love him is a gift, no matter how it ends. You do it, too, you know. Maybe in a different way, but you sacrifice your peace of mind every time you begin to care for one of your patients."

"I don't see that it's the same, at all, but thank you. Now, about the horseback riding," he began.

She shot him a warning look. "I got approval from the specialist. It won't damage his spine and it might help as the muscles in his core get stronger and support the spine better."

Ash sighed, a long, drawn out, patient sigh. "Are you finished?"

She cut her eyes at him. "Maybe. I'm not sure until you say whatever it is you're going to say next."

"I was just about to say that now that he's on horseback, maybe we need to get him a gait trainer, like a walker for kids with special needs. It might be the next logical step toward getting him on his feet."

Jordan grabbed his face and planted a kiss on his lips, then looked away, her fair skin flushing bright red. "You're the best. I'll talk to the physiologist next time we see him."

The screen door on Claire's back porch slammed open. "Aunt J! Levi wants you to see his cookies."

"Time to get my sugared-up kid home for a bath. See you later?"

"Thursday night is the fund-raiser."

Jordan turned back. "I haven't forgotten, if you still want me to go with you."

"Just try to get out of it."

She left him swinging under the oak tree, as the sun started to sink in the sky, wondering how in the world she always managed to wrap him in knots.

Chapter Ten

The midnight blue silk looked ridiculous hanging in her closet next to her flannel shirts. Jordan stood in her robe in front of her closet and wished, for the thousandth time, that she hadn't said yes to Ash's request. Ash's sister Wynn had been recruited to help Jordan get ready. In her flowy tunic, cropped leggings and flats, she looked more chic than Jordan had ever looked in her life. Unlike Jordan's frizzy curls, Wynn's straight blond hair wouldn't dare be out of place. "What are you doing? We're behind schedule. Come on, it's hair and makeup time."

Jordan followed her into the front room. "You really don't have to do this. The dress is enough."

"Sit."

Jordan sat. And felt like an idiot. "I ride horses. I shovel horse manure. I don't go to black-tie events. What was he thinking?"

Wynn's hand stilled in her hair and picked back up again. "Maybe he was thinking that he likes you and wants to spend time with you."

Jordan's stomach was so jittery, she felt like she could throw up at any minute. "We're just friends."

"I know. Don't move. I don't want to burn you with this thing." Wynn worked with a flat iron to smooth all of the unruly curls in Jordan's hair.

"He's not my type. He wore loafers in the barn to muck out a stall." She looked up at Wynn. "Loafers."

Wynn's eyebrows drew up in a quizzical V. "Are you trying to convince yourself or me?"

"I don't know." And that was the truth. Ash had turned out to be so much more than she thought he was in the beginning.

Their lifestyle was light-years apart. But he was in the barn in loafers because he wanted to help her, even though horses weren't his favorite thing.

Wynn twisted Jordan's mass of red hair into a low knot and used about a million pins to secure it. Digging around in her bag, she came up with a rhinestone clip and slid it into place just behind Jordan's ear. Jordan squirmed.

Wynn rapped her on the shoulder. "I said don't move. I have to spray it."

"You're so bossy. I want to see."

"Not yet. we're going to do your makeup first."

Jordan blinked. "I wasn't really planning on makeup."

"Mmm-hmm," Wynn murmured, a couple of makeup brushes clamped between her teeth.

Ash's sister brushed and dabbed, using pots and compacts and stuff Jordan had never heard of. "Are all those products really necessary?"

"Yes, your skin looks like porcelain. Every girl there is going to be jealous."

People were going to be looking at her skin? Once

again, her nervous stomach threatened revolt. "I don't know if I can do this."

Wynn laughed, tapped some blush off the brush and applied it to the apples of Jordan's cheeks. "Stop whining. In DC I used to go to a couple of these things a week. It's for a good cause, so buck up."

Desperate to direct the conversation away from her complexion, Jordan asked, "Did you always want to live in Washington, DC?"

When she answered, Wynn's voice was soft. "I used to think I could make a difference. I wanted to work for the people. Now close your eyes."

Obediently, Jordan closed them. "And you came home because…?"

Silence.

Jordan opened her eyes again. "If it's none of my business, just tell me to shut up."

Wynn didn't tell her to shut up. She just looked sad, her beautiful Sheehan-blue eyes dark with misery. "Mostly I realized how naive I was. I set out to change the world and I think the only thing that changed was me. Okay! We're done and it only took twenty minutes."

Jordan grinned. "That's only about nineteen minutes longer than my usual beauty routine. I want to see."

Wynn smiled. "Dress first."

The dress Wynn had brought over for her was a body-hugging column of blue silk. Wynn zipped her into it and took a step back. "You look amazing. One more thing." Wynn reached into her bag and pulled out an enormous diamond on a thin platinum chain.

Jordan goggled. "I can't borrow that."

"Please. It would make me very happy for you to wear it."

When Jordan looked into the mirror, she didn't recognize herself. Her eyes looked enormous, her lips a pale natural pink that somehow looked like a luscious pout. "Whoa, you're a magician."

Wynn laughed. "You gave me a lot to work with. Next time we're doing your eyebrows."

Jordan's hands shot up to cover her brows. "What do you mean, *do* them? It's going to be painful, isn't it?"

Wynn laughed. "Yes."

A car door slammed outside and Jordan's chest quivered, nerves back in full force. "He's here."

"I'll check on Levi and make sure he's got everything he needs to spend the night at the big house." Wynn turned back at the door. "Jordan, please have fun. You deserve it."

As the door closed behind Wynn, Jordan tried to pace and almost ended up in a heap on the floor. How did people walk in these stilts?

Ash knocked. She closed her eyes and took a deep breath. She could do this.

She opened the door and her knees went weak. He was in a slim black tuxedo and, on his arm, a dozen yellow roses.

She was the hay girl, the barn chick, a tomboy if there ever was one. No one had ever brought her flowers before. She never knew she wanted them to.

His slightly stunned expression brought a laugh bubbling to the surface. She blinked back the tears that would ruin her mascara. No way in the world she was letting that happen.

* * *

The room was small, smaller than Jordan had expected, decorated with life-size artificial trees twinkling with fairy lights. Each table had a crisp white cloth and a towering arrangement of white roses.

Ash's hand skimmed the small of her back. "This group has been getting together for this event for more than a hundred years. It's one of the oldest civic groups in the nation. It's made up of some of the most influential movers and shakers in the region. Every year they choose a handful of nonprofits to highlight. This dinner is to recognize the finalists and the one they've chosen to support this year. It's a huge honor."

They were seated at a table near the front of the room. One of the other couples at the table happened to be the parents of one of Jordan's favorite clients. She knew Audrey and Nic Caravelo as parents and enjoyed getting to know them on a more personal level. Audrey was a talented photographer and Nic had a wicked sense of humor that almost made her forget where she was and how nervous she was.

Ash, however, wouldn't let her forget. His talented doctor fingers were seemingly everywhere—her bare shoulder, her neck, offering her a taste of his steak, which by itself was almost enough to make her willingly return to another of these fancy soirees.

When the waitstaff had cleared the dinner dishes and placed decadent plates of chocolate mousse cake at each place, an elderly gentleman stepped to the podium. "I'm Edgar Rochester. As most of you know, my grandfather started this organization over a hundred years ago. He spent his life amassing a fortune and by the end of it, he wanted to share that fortune with the people who had spent their lives making other people's lives better."

The giant screen over the podium began flashing photographs of the nonprofits being honored tonight. Her heart touched, Jordan sat there with a lump in her throat as she watched. She knew the kind of work that went into a successful nonprofit. There was one dedicated to creating handicap-friendly playgrounds and one supporting retired working dogs. The next two were both organizations that worked with the homeless population and then…a picture of her flashed on the screen.

She gulped. She hadn't known it was being taken but that wasn't unusual. Parents loved to have photos of their kids on horseback. But her picture was there, on the screen, not sitting in one of her clients' living rooms on the end table. She whirled on Ash. "What is this?"

He held both hands up, but a huge grin covered his face. "I didn't do it."

"I did," Audrey said.

Jordan was so confused, color rushing to her face, her heart beating double-time. "I don't understand."

"You will." Audrey patted her hand as Edgar Rochester's voice boomed from the speakers.

"Each of our honorees will be receiving ten thousand dollars to use in their organizations, and the winner of the Rochester Award will be granted an additional fifty-thousand-dollar grant. And now I'd like to call Audrey Caravelo to introduce our Rochester Award winner."

Jordan's stomach tilted, that fancy meal sitting like lead. She forgot to breathe.

Audrey made her way to the podium, dark eyes and

sleek black hair offset by the pale pink of her dress. "I'd like to start by telling you a story about a little boy…"

By the time Audrey finished the story about her son's struggle with autism, half the room was in tears, including Jordan. Her mascara was a mess.

A new picture flashed on screen—this one of Audrey's son, Evan, on Jordan's horse, Leo, with a huge smile on his face. Audrey smiled, too, but her eyes swam with tears. "Jordan Conley, you and your horses work wonders. I never thought I would hear Evan say my name or tell me he loves me or even ask for a drink of water, but he does all those things because you and Leo unlocked it for him. You gave him confidence and you helped his overloaded system begin to work together. I can't thank you enough for the change you have brought to my son."

She looked around the room. "It is my distinct pleasure to announce this year's Rochester Award Winner, Jordan Conley, from Horses, Hope and Healing."

As Jordan stood, she was absolutely stunned that the applause continued as one after the other of those in attendance got to their feet. She managed the walk to the podium only by deliberately placing one foot in front of the other.

Swiping at tears, praying she didn't have raccoon eyes, she stopped in front of the room, shifting awkwardly in the borrowed high heels.

Audrey caught her in a tight hug and whispered in her ear, "You deserve this."

The award was a small tasteful crystal bowl. It shot points of fire from the lights trained on the podium as

Jordan held it in her hands. The crystal was beautiful but it paled in comparison to Jordan.

She was absolutely radiant.

Ash was thunderstruck.

On a normal day, Jordan had a certain fresh-faced beauty, made all the more powerful because she was so completely unaware of it. Tonight he had trouble forming words.

She smiled, looking out at the small crowd. "I never imagined when I agreed to come to a boring fund-raiser that it could be so exciting and overwhelming. And I truly never imagined that you would honor me in such a generous way. From the time I was a teenager, I dreamed about using horses to help kids who struggled in traditional therapy. I'm so excited for what the future holds for Triple H and incredibly grateful that you chose my organization to honor tonight. Thank you so much."

She shook the hand of the elderly Mr. Rochester and made her way back to the seat beside Ash. Her perfume, something exotic he'd never noticed before, wound around him. He was so proud of her and humbled to be able to be a part—albeit a small part—of her life and mission.

After the other honorees were introduced, the evening was adjourned. She spent another half hour accepting congratulations. Ash spoke to a few people, but after a few minutes eased away from the crowd around Jordan.

He was used to seeing her in her work clothes. Braids and flannel looked good on her. But tonight, watching her as she circled the room, making sure to speak to everyone, she was staggeringly beautiful.

It wasn't the hair or makeup or dress, either, although those things were fine. It was her courage, her passion, her heart, that shone out of her.

When the group of people finally thinned, she looked around for him. He knew when she saw him. Her eyes locked with his and a slow smile spread across her face. She walked toward him. "Hi."

"Hi, yourself. You ready to get out of here?"

"So ready. These shoes are killing me."

He laughed and offered his arm.

In minutes, she was in the passenger seat of his cushy black car and they drove away from the lights and the people. He glanced over at her. "Are you tired?"

"A little. Also a little wired. Did you know they were going to do that? Of course you did, you jerk." She laughed when she answered her own question.

"Audrey wanted it to be a surprise. You have a powerful ally there. What are you going to do with the grant money?"

She didn't hesitate. "Build a covered arena. Right now if the weather's bad, we have to cancel sessions. It's really disruptive for the kids."

"I want to show you something," he said, turning onto a dirt road. "Not even my family has been out here. It's been my secret."

"I feel honored."

"You should. It's my get-away-from-the-world spot." At the end of the drive, a house sat on a bluff.

"Whose house is this?"

Ash glanced at her and back to the bumpy road. "It's mine. It's under construction. It wasn't in livable condition when I bought it, but the house isn't why I bought the property."

He opened the car door for her and held her hand as she got out. Somewhere along the way, she'd ditched the heels. He didn't go into the house, instead grabbing a battery-operated lantern from the trunk.

Taking her hand, he walked with her closer to the edge, where they could see the dark ribbon of the river winding through the ravine. "Sometimes I come out here to sit and just listen. Life's hardships seem far away out here."

"I think I can see a million stars." Her voice was husky smoke.

He slid his arm around her waist, his fingers skimming across the smooth silk, and tugged her closer. For a minute he closed his eyes, just breathing her in, swaying in the moonlight to the music of the river.

His voice was a rough whisper against her ear. "I didn't ask you to the dinner tonight because I knew you were being honored. I did—know, I mean—but I asked you because I wanted to be with you away from the farm, away from the hospital and the day-to-day pressures."

She didn't say anything, just laid her head in the hollow of his shoulder.

He cleared his throat. "I know you think I'm not the relationship type. And that's okay—I haven't been. Ever since a close friend of mine died in high school, I've had this attitude. Life is short. Live it. Expend it. Go down in flames on empty. I kind of feel like I'm living her life, too. I don't know if that makes sense at all."

Jordan stopped swaying and lifted her head to look into his eyes, hers dark and luminous in the light of the moon. "It does. I'm so sorry about your friend."

"Thank you." He skimmed his fingers down the

curve of her neck. "Jordan, I've never had a relationship because since Victoria died, I never found anyone
that I wanted to have one with, not really. I watched
you tonight, after the dinner. You share that bright
light that's in you with everyone you meet. With me.
I don't know what to do with that kind of generosity."

"I don't know what to say."

"Say you'll give this a chance. Say you like me. Say
whatever it is you're feeling."

"Oh, Ash. I'm just a farm girl and for this one night
I've gotten to be the princess. You brought me flowers."

"You are so much more than a farm girl." He slid
his hand around to cup her neck and lowered his mouth
to hers, letting all the feelings he'd tried to suppress
over the past months pour into that one simple gesture.

He didn't know what the future held, and right now
he didn't care. It was this moment that mattered.

Her arms slipped around his neck and he pulled
her closer. He didn't want to waste a moment of the
moonlight.

Chapter Eleven

It was after midnight when Ash pulled the car into the driveway and turned off the ignition. Jordan's head was spinning with everything that had happened. The awards dinner, the civic group's incredible generosity to Triple H and, most of all, the time with Ash at the river.

They sat for a moment with the car ticking in the silence.

Because the kiss on the riverbank was what her mind lingered on, she rambled. "I had a really nice time tonight. I have to admit that I felt like an idiot getting all dressed up. And those shoes. Well, the shoes were as bad as I thought they'd be, but the party wasn't. The people were amazing. The award. I don't know what to think about that, still."

"It was a really great night. But next time we go on a date, maybe you pick the place." His phone buzzed and she wondered who it was contacting him after midnight, but he cleared it from his screen without a glance. "I can walk you to the door."

She shook her head. "I'm going in to check on Levi before I hit the bed at my place."

Before she could get out, he had his door open and was around the car opening hers. He held a hand out. She slid her fingers into his and stood, the torture-shoes dangling from her other hand.

His eyes were on hers, a mischievous, flirtatious look that she knew she would be thinking about after he left. His lips were inches—millimeters, really—away from hers. Her breath caught as he ran a single slim finger down her jawline. "I'll see you tomorrow."

She held his gaze, wishing she could see inside that quick, agile mind. "Okay."

Brushing past him with a rustle of blue silk, she walked up the steps and into the house. She leaned back against the door, her eyes closed. What a night.

"About time you got home."

The shoes hit the floor. "Claire? What are you doing lurking in here?"

Her twin sat up on the couch. "Waiting on you. Yoga pants in the powder room. Ice cream in the freezer. I want details."

Jordan found the stretchy black pants and an over-size T-shirt in the bathroom and slid into them with no small amount of relief. Claire had even left a padded hanger on the hook on the back of the door for the dress.

Grabbing the tub of ice cream from the freezer, she dropped onto the couch beside her sister and passed her a spoon. She dug it into the rocky road and looked into Claire's expectant face. "It was the most horribly boring evening I've ever had. I can't believe you all talked me into going."

Claire's face fell and a half second later, she was laughing. "You almost had me. But you won an award that came with fifty thousand dollars tonight. That's not boring."

Another spoon of ice cream and a sigh. "It was magical. I can't even believe I'm saying that because I had on a formal dress and killer heels for hours, but it was just one of those nights that was…perfect."

"You got home awfully late." Claire mumbled with her mouth full.

"We might've sat by the river to look at the stars." Ash's property and plans were his secret to share when he was ready to share it.

Claire squealed, abruptly dropping her voice to a whisper when there was murmured movement from the bedroom down the hall. "Was there kissing? Please tell me there was kissing."

Jordan didn't say anything, but her fair skin gave her away every time. She took another bite of ice cream and willed her cheeks to stop burning.

Her twin sister shot to her feet, dancing a little boogie, which was hilarious considering she was five months pregnant. "I am such a genius. I knew, *knew*, you guys would hit it off when I asked Ash to hang out with you and help you with Levi."

Jordan stopped laughing when she realized what Claire had just said, a knot forming in her stomach. Her sister had asked Ash to spend time with her?

She put her spoon down. "I'm gonna run upstairs and check on Levi and then I'm going to bed. Can I leave Levi here until tomorrow?"

Claire stopped dancing and searched Jordan's face. "Of course. You can stay here, too, if you want."

Jordan went upstairs to what they thought of as the toddler room. There were three little toddler beds in a row, each with cartoon character bedding. She stepped over the gate in the doorway and knelt down by Levi's bed. He was sleeping soundly, his hand lying open. She brushed a finger down his cheek and he smiled in his sleep before turning over to burrow into the covers.

Sweet boy.

She went back down the stairs and into the kitchen, where Claire was putting the ice cream into the freezer.

"Are you all right? Did I say something?"

Forcing a smile, Jordan picked up the hanger with the borrowed dress. "I'm fine. It just hit me how tired I am. I'll see you in the morning. Thanks for the ice cream."

She closed the door quietly behind her and headed for her cottage. The water of the pond was still tonight. The same stars she'd felt like a princess under just hours ago glistening in the surface.

Was what she'd felt for Ash real?

The smart, funny girl ends up with the cutest guy in town. It was straight out of a romantic comedy, but did it happen in real life?

Not to people like her. Hadn't she had that very thought?

She'd told Claire she was exhausted and she'd been telling the truth. She let Gus out and took the opportunity to go into the bathroom and wash the makeup off her face. Maybe she'd enjoyed it a little, being someone else, someone a little prettier, someone with a little more polish, but as her freckles appeared, she knew that person wasn't who she was.

When Gus came back and let her know with a deep

low bark that he was waiting, she let him in and went straight to bed.

Gus jumped up beside her, which he never did. He knew he wasn't allowed on the bed. He shimmy-crawled until he was lying next to her and she put her arm around him.

On her bedside table, her cell phone buzzed. Message from Claire.

She ignored it. It wasn't like her, but she didn't want to get into it with her sister, not until she had time to process. Right now she was leading with hurt. Once upon a time, she'd been the sick twin, the unwanted one. Rejected first by her biological parents and then by adoptive parents before their mom adopted them both together. This situation felt like a new wound on top of some old scar tissue.

Maybe that was melodramatic. Okay, it *was* melodramatic and she knew it, but she wanted Ash to want to spend time with her because he liked her, not because her twin sister asked him to.

Her heart ached as she went over every second of the evening in her head. Had she imagined the connection?

It had seemed real.

She buried her fingers in Gus's thick fur. Maybe tomorrow she could sort through her feelings and let the hurt go.

Or maybe not.

Ash pulled to a stop in the driveway at Red Hill Farm. He had no excuse for being there, other than a flat of zinnias in the back seat, which he bought because they reminded him of Jordan. They were hardy little flowers but incredibly bright. They made him happy just looking at them.

And yeah, he was fully aware that it was a silly gesture, but there was something about Jordan that made him feel a little silly and romantic.

He dropped the flowers and a half-empty bottle of water off on her porch and set out to look for Jordan. He found her outside the equipment shed, tinkering and muttering as she worked on the engine of the ATV she used to drag the area where she held therapy sessions. "Hey, what's going on?"

Jordan looked up, scowled and rubbed sweat off her forehead with a gloved hand, leaving a swipe of dirt behind. "I've got a wire connected to the ignition that's chafed and frayed. The thing won't start."

"I can get Joe's truck and trailer and help you get it to the repair place." The look she gave him could have withered those zinnias instantly.

She blew the hair off her face. "I'm not some airhead who depends on other people to do everything. I never said I couldn't fix it." Soldering gun in hand, she leaned over the engine again.

"Airhead?"

She went still for a second then looked at him sideways, still bent over the engine. "Give me the electrical tape."

He handed it to her and she turned back to the wire she was repairing.

"I, ah, I think I'm going to go see what Joe and the kids are up to."

Her voice was muffled. "See ya later."

It had been a whim to come out here when he saw the bright-colored zinnias. He was happy. Happy flowers. Now he was wondering if he'd made a big mistake. She hadn't exactly reciprocated after he shared his feelings last night.

Maybe she'd just been caught up. The moonlight, stars, scent of honeysuckle heavy in the air. It was a heady mix. So maybe it was understandable if she was having second thoughts. Maybe?

Her gardening tools, the small ones, were in a bucket on her front porch. He picked up the trowel and spade and began to plant the flowers he brought her in the beds right beside the steps to her cottage, where she would see them every day.

"Hey, Uncle Ash. Whatcha doin'?" His thirteen-year-old niece, Amelia, was sprawled on the steps the way only a long-limbed teenager could do. "I brought you a Popsicle."

He squinted his eyes at it. "It looks good but I probably shouldn't."

"It's made out of fruit, no sugar. And Claire has pretty much banned food coloring, so there's none of that, either."

Amused, Ash took the dripping Popsicle and bit into it. It tasted weird.

"There might be sweet potatoes in it. She throws all the leftovers in the blender and makes smoothie Popsicles."

Gross. "Oh…yum. Healthy Popsicles."

"So why are you planting flowers?"

He grinned. "I saw them and thought Jordan would like them."

"You crushin' on Aunt Jordan?"

"I don't know. I guess. She was a little cranky when

I talked to her a few minutes ago, though, so I don't think she's *crushing* on me back."

Amelia shrugged one slim shoulder. "I don't know. My dad always says if a guy is mean to you that means they probably like you and don't want anyone to know."

Ash sat back on his heels. He was going to have to have a talk with Joe about what kind of advice he was giving his daughter about guys, but in this case, it was worth a thought. Maybe last night was overwhelming for Jordan and she didn't know how to react to him today. It didn't necessarily mean she wasn't on the same wavelength.

Maybe she did like him. Or maybe she didn't and she just didn't know how to tell him.

He scowled at the flowers.

His niece finished off her Popsicle and stuck the stick in the back pocket of her cutoffs. "Personally, I think if a guy is mean to you, you should punch 'im in the face. Life's too short."

"Agreed. I mean, no. Punching people is not allowed. But you're right. Life's too short." With considerable effort, Ash held in his laughter until Amelia was well away from Jordan's cottage. He called after her. "Thanks for the treat."

She threw one arm in the air in response and the laugh rolled out. Amelia had been dropped by her mom on his brother's doorstep as an angry, undernourished kid with no idea what a real family looked like. Joe, and then Claire, too, had been showing her love every day since and she had turned into a feisty, confident kid he adored.

He patted the dirt down around the last little flower and sat on the porch steps, leaning back on one elbow, taking a swig from his bottle of water. Jordan said last night that her evening had been magical, but she never said she shared his feelings or that she was falling for him, too.

He felt like an idiot, but he guessed the biggest question was where did he go from here? Did he chuck the whole idea or did he fight for her?

His mother, Bertie, had a saying: Love is always worth it.

If that was true, he only had one choice.

Jordan finished dragging the ring where they did the therapy sessions and put the ATV back into the shed. She grabbed the hand rake on her way out the door. There were a few spots that she'd had trouble getting to with the drag and she would break those up by hand.

The horses were turned out to pasture today. She'd seen them cavorting and rolling and having a good time earlier this morning. It had warmed up now and they were sleepily grazing on the far side of the pasture.

When she rounded the corner of the barn, she saw Joe. He'd gotten the hose and sprayer out of the barn and was wetting down the top layer, which would've been her next job. "Hey, thanks."

He looked up. "It's nap time inside and I saw you out here working so I thought I might give you a hand. Nice day. A little sunshine, you know."

"I appreciate it."

"No problem. I heard y'all had a good time last night."

All the good feelings she'd had toward Joe for helping her evaporated. She narrowed her eyes. "Who'd you hear that from?"

Joe studied her face for a minute and calmly continued watering while she slammed the rake into the clumps of clay and sand. "You won an award, I heard."

Either Joe was smart enough to avoid her question or he was actually interested in the award. Either way, the award was a much safer topic than the fact that she'd been kissing his brother in the moonlight last night.

She grinned. "Fifty-thousand-dollar grant and the first thing on the list is a covered arena. We'll still have to pick and drag and water, but we can work in all weather, and have space enough to do some really awesome things with our therapy sessions."

"And you and Ash had a good time? Wynn said you looked really beautiful, which I don't have a hard time believing."

So apparently her brother-in-law wasn't interested in sticking to safe topics. "I had a good time."

Joe glanced up as she stabbed viciously at a hard clump of clay. He cleared his throat. "Jordan, I'm not going to ask about what happened last night, good or bad. That's between you and Ash."

She eased off on the rake a bit, but then he kept talking.

"You know, it's no secret that I had a rough childhood. I cheated, fought, lied, stole...whatever it took. I can't imagine how my mom could look at me and see that there was something worth working for on the inside." He wasn't looking at Jordan now, but they worked side by side.

"I love your mom."

"Yeah, me, too. The way I see it, finding love with someone is a risk-reward scenario."

She paused in the raking. "I'm not sure I'm following you."

"Is it a risk to put yourself out there and possibly get no return? Or worse, humiliation? Yeah, of course it is. When I took my messed up ten-year-old self to live with my family, I risked everything. But so did they. Luckily, it worked, but even if it hadn't, it was worth the risk because the reward was so great."

She drew in a breath and leaned on the rake handle. "I really can't stand you right now."

Joe's laugh burst out, a deep rolling chuckle. "I also almost lost Claire because I wasn't willing to change my plans to make room for her in my life. Look at everything I would be missing if I hadn't come to my senses."

He walked closer, so close she could see herself in those mirrored sunglasses he wore all the time. "Ash is a good-looking man—or so I hear—but despite that, he's one of the best people I know. I hope that you won't treat him carelessly."

"I'm not gonna—" She paused, frustrated with herself and Joe and a little mad and she couldn't even put her finger on the why. "I gotta go. Thanks for your help with the watering."

She stalked out of the ring and down the trail to the shed, tossing the rake in before stomping away. Who did he think he was? She made it about six paces before she turned around, picked up the rake and hung it in its place on the wall of the shed.

Still nursing the anger, or hurt, she wasn't sure which, she rounded the corner by her house and stopped cold. There were three perfectly neat rows of bright-colored flowers—hot pink, orange, yellow—on either side of her porch steps.

Amelia was a few feet away with one of the younger kids, throwing rocks into the pond.

"Hey, Amelia, who planted these?"

Her niece glanced over. "Uncle Ash. He was here a while ago."

"I know. I just didn't know he… Never mind." She'd been stewing over the fact that Claire had set up this whole thing and he'd been planting flowers in front of her house.

"He said he got them because he thought you'd like them. Ha! Mine skipped three times!"

"I do like them." She said it to herself. And she liked Ash, too. Risk vs. reward; that was what Joe said. Her eyebrows drew together in a frown. She wasn't risk averse. She'd moved here, hadn't she?

Could she admit to herself that she was afraid of taking a chance on a relationship? Afraid of putting herself out there and getting rejected?

Ash was gorgeous and smart and—she looked at the zinnias—sweet, too. Last night *had* been magical, and by doubting it, she was dissing him and he didn't deserve that.

She needed to make it right.

Chapter Twelve

Little by little, with Latham's help, Ash was making progress on the house on the bluff. When he bought the property, he only had thoughts for the view. His plan had been to get anything salvageable out of it, tear the rest down and start over, eventually.

But then he'd found a photograph of the house when it was new, over a hundred years ago. A young couple sat on the porch steps with their child crawling in the grass in front of them. He'd decided right then to renovate the house. It had raised a family, had a history and real character, the kind you couldn't get in a new build.

He hadn't planned to work out here today, but he needed to burn off some energy after the conversation with Jordan and put it out of his mind for a little while. For that, he needed muscle straining, seriously sweaty work on the deck. It was the only place Latham would let him work without supervision.

He laid a pressure-treated board in place and hammered nails into it every twelve inches or so. The zing up his arm when the hammer hit the nail was extremely satisfying.

Wheels spinning on the dirt road leading to his place caught his attention. He was enough off the beaten path that people didn't come here by accident. He grabbed a drink out of the mini cooler on the porch and walked around the corner of the house.

Jordan was pulling to a stop in her old farm truck. He didn't smile. She'd gotten under his skin, made him feel things he never expected to feel and slammed the door on him with no warning.

No work-stained clothes this time, when she got out of the truck. She wore slim dark jeans and a loose-fitting scoop-neck T-shirt, her long auburn hair loose and lifting in the soft breeze off the river.

In contrast, he was sweaty and filthy from the construction work in the house, and the juxtaposition made him cranky. "Can I help you?"

Jordan slid Wayfarer sunglasses off her face. "I owe you an apology."

He looked right into those sea-colored eyes and didn't respond. "Okay."

She glanced out at the river, where the sun still sparkled in the late-afternoon sun. "I don't even have an excuse. Claire told me last night that she set all this up, that she asked you to hang out with me and help with Levi. I guess it made me wonder whether what happened was even real." Her voice was barely above a whisper. "Whether what you felt was real."

Ash shoved his fingers into his hair, and dirt and dust rained down. "I'm not sure what to say. I didn't see it that way. Claire asked me to meet you at the hospital and check on Levi that first night because she couldn't be there. I didn't think she was trying to set us up."

"She was, but it doesn't matter." She took a step

toward him, her hand slightly outstretched. "It's me that's the problem, not Claire. Not you."

He sighed. "Do you want to come sit down and have a drink?"

She nodded and he led her to the porch and two rusty metal porch chairs. Pulling another drink out of the cooler, he handed it to her. "Sorry it's diet. It's all I have."

"It's okay." She cracked it and took a drink and held it in her two hands. "Look, this is going to be embarrassing, but I have to say it. You're handsome. I mean gorgeous, really, and smart. The whole package. I look at you and I get tongue-tied. At least I did, before I got to know you better. So in my mind, there was a huge gap between me and the kind of woman that you usually go for."

He raised an eyebrow. "Airheads?"

She flushed, her cheeks turning pink. "Yeah, sorry about that."

He laughed softly. "It's okay. Can I talk now?"

"No. I'm not finished yet." But her eyes warmed on his. "So when we started hanging out because of Levi, I started to see a different side of you, one I didn't know was there behind all the shine, you know?"

He shrugged and thought, *Not really.* "I guess."

This time, she rolled her eyes. "You have to know how people see you. All those moms don't dress up to go to Dr. Harvey to get their teeth cleaned."

"Ew." Ash had a momentary image of his seventy-year-old dentist and a waiting room full of women in tennis skirts. He pushed the image out of his mind to focus on what was important: Jordan. "All that stuff doesn't mean anything to me."

"I know that. Now." She looked away, shook her head as her eyes filled. "But when Claire told me last night that she set us up, my first thought was that you were seeing me as a favor to her. Today I woke up feeling hurt and I took it out on you and…I'm so sorry."

He'd come over to the house to work off his frustration. The dirty, hot work had gone a long way to making him feel better. The apology and explanation from Jordan took him the rest of the way. He got to his feet, walked over to her slowly and stuck out a grimy hand, laughing when she didn't hesitate.

"I'm gonna talk now, okay?" Pulling her to her feet, he eased her closer. "You don't give yourself enough credit, Jordan. You have me so besotted with you that I brought you flowers today because they reminded me of you." He tilted her face up toward his and kissed her gently on the lips. "Let's just take it one day at a time."

"Yes, okay." She nodded. "Okay. The flowers are really beautiful."

"I'm glad you like them." The sun was starting to dip in the sky and Ash realized he hadn't eaten in hours. His phone was in the house and the app connected to his glucose monitor was probably going nuts. He needed his test kit and to eat as soon as possible.

He hated to talk about being a diabetic and didn't, as a rule, talk about it with women he was dating. Jordan was different. And if he wanted their whatever-this-was to work, maybe there should be different ground rules, like honesty, no matter what.

Clearing his throat, he said, "Hey, I just realized how late it is. I'd better go in and test my glucose."

"Okay, I have to go, anyway. I'm paying Mrs. Matthews for an extra hour, but it's time for me to pick Levi up." She pressed a quick kiss to his lips and bounded down the stairs, before turning back. "I'll see you later."

As he walked into the house, he heard the old engine of the farm truck fire up and bump down the dirt lane. She wasn't like anyone else he knew. Beautiful, yes. Smart, yes. But there was something else. Maybe it was the therapy work she did, or maybe it was her background.

He pulled out his test kit and cleaned his finger with an alcohol swab so he could prick it. He'd dated a lot of women casually, a lot of beautiful women even, but Jordan was special. She didn't even blink when he'd told her he was going in to check his glucose level.

He drew in a breath as he programmed his insulin pump. He wasn't a good bet for the long haul. He should probably tell her that.

But maybe not yet. Right now he didn't want to be a cancer survivor or someone living with diabetes; he just wanted to be a man who was falling in love with a woman.

Jordan knocked on the back door at Red Hill Farm and felt like an idiot. She hadn't ever knocked, not even once.

Claire pulled the door open, a small knife in her hand and Sweetness in a baby carrier strapped to her chest. Hurt hid in her eyes.

Before either of them could say anything, Levi, in a high chair at the island, said, "Mama! Hey, Mama!"

She crossed to her sweet little man and gave him a big kiss. "Hey, buddy, did you have fun today?"

He grinned up at her and pointed to his plate. "Happy."

Jordan glanced up at Mrs. Matthews, who smiled. "He made a happy plate. He ate grapes and chicken nuggets and a few pieces of carrot."

"Big boy." Jordan sat on the bar stool next to Levi, across from Claire, who was chopping more carrots and not looking at her. "I owe you an apology, Claire."

Mrs. Matthews dried her hands on a dish towel. "I'm going to make sure those twins are doing their homework. Half the time they end up wrestling on the floor."

Jordan waited until Mrs. Matthews had gone before she said, "I was really upset with you last night, and I was wrong."

Claire stopped chopping and met her eyes with a cool blue look. "Go on."

"When I went to the awards dinner with Ash, I felt like a different person. I was wearing Wynn's dress and Wynn's makeup and my hair was all done. And those shoes." She shook her head as she squirted more ketchup onto Levi's plate. "And then there was the kissing."

"That sounds promising."

Jordan stared at her sister. "Seriously, stop. This is hard enough."

Blue eyes dancing with laughter now, Claire tried and failed to keep a straight face. "Okay, really. I'm fine. Go on."

"This is my deal, okay? It sounds like I'm jealous of you or mad at you or whatever, but I'm not." She pinched the bridge of her nose. "I'm just making this worse. Okay, so I've always kind of felt like I held you back, that you were healthy and beautiful and perfect and I was just the tagalong twin."

Claire stopped laughing. "Jordan."

"Even when I moved here—you had the idea for this place, the whole plan. I was the tagalong again."

Her sister was shaking her head. "You inherited half of the property just like I did. This place is half yours."

"I know. I do. But this is about how I felt, not what's really true. You know what I mean?"

"Yes. I think so."

Jordan picked up a paper towel, smoothed it. "So, fast-forward to last night and here I am after a night that seemed like it was out of a dream and then I found out that you set the whole thing up. So in my mind, I felt like the tagalong sister again."

Claire had tears in her eyes now. "I never, ever meant for you to feel that way. I did think you and Ash would get along, but he didn't hang out with you all this time because I asked him to."

"I know that now. And if I had stopped to really think about it, I probably would have come to the same conclusion. I just had to work through it." She picked up one of the pieces of carrot from Levi's plate and put it down again. "I had to apologize to Ash, too. I was a real pain to everyone. I'm sorry."

Levi looked at his ketchup-covered fingers and, instead of reaching for the paper towel she held out to him, dried them off in his hair. "Oh, yuck, Levi. Let's wipe them off."

Jordan grabbed a baby wipe from the box on the island and started to work on Levi's sticky fingers.

Her sister came around the island and put her arms around Jordan. "I don't know why you're the only person who can't see how amazing you are."

"I don't know. Maybe because that would be weird?"

Levi held up his arms and Jordan picked him up. "I have to get this little dude home and in the bath."

"Bath?" His big brown eyes lit up.

"Yes, my man. You have ketchup in your hair."

"Bath." He wrapped his arms around her neck. "Mama."

"Mama J," she corrected automatically as she hugged him tight.

Claire smiled at him. "He's picking up new words all the time. It won't be long and he'll be caught up with his peers. Hey, I almost forgot. Can you do me a favor? Joe has this regional chief of police thing tomorrow night and spouses are supposed to come. I wondered if you could help Mrs. Matthews out?"

"Yeah, of course."

"I figured she could handle it with Amelia and Kiera, but there's a slight possibility that Penny's older brother might be moving here tomorrow, so I want her to have some backup."

"Is this the same brother they said might be coming a couple of weeks ago?"

"Yes." Claire picked up the carrots and dumped them into a bowlful of lettuce. "I know they want them together, but I don't know what the holdup is. Bureaucracy. Whatever. If he comes, there's a bed open in the room next to the twins."

"Okay, no problem. I think my last session of the day will be over at four thirty but I'll check to be sure."

"Thanks."

Levi had melted into Jordan's arms, his head heavy on her shoulder. "I better get this kid home and in the bath before he goes to sleep."

Her hand was on the doorknob when her sister called her name. She turned around.

"Jordan, I love you. The work you do is important. And as for me, I couldn't survive without you and that's the truth."

Something loosened inside and Jordan took a deep breath. "Thanks."

She opened the door and stepped into the sunshine with Levi.

Thunder rocked the old house, but no less than the raucous voices of eight, no, make that nine, counting Levi, kids trapped inside by a late-evening thunderstorm.

The youngest baby was strapped into her high chair, but wailing. The six-year-old was bouncing down the stairs in a sleeping bag—on purpose.

Kiera was at the kitchen table with earphones in, trying to do homework. Her baby was asleep in the swing beside her—though Jordan couldn't imagine sleeping through this racket—and Amelia was sick in bed with strep throat.

Jordan had taken one look at Mrs. Matthews's glassy eyes and sent her home for the night after making her promise that she, too, would go to the doctor in the morning for some antibiotics.

Approximately thirty minutes after her arrival, she found the twins painting the downstairs bathroom with shaving cream. God only knew where they found it but every square inch of the bathroom was covered in it, including themselves.

So, what did a smart babysitter do? She called in reinforcements.

Ash arrived ten minutes later. He came through the back door, shaking water from his hair and rolling up his sleeves. "Where do you need me?"

She handed Levi to him and tried not to burst into tears of gratitude. "Tag team?"

"You got it."

A handful of puffs dried the tears on Sweetness's little face. She tapped Kiera on the shoulder. "Leaving Sweetness with you. I'll be right back."

Next up were the identical twins, Jamie and John, who were in the bathroom "cleaning" the mess they made earlier.

Ash grinned. "I got this one."

He pushed opened the door to the bathroom and shouted over them. "Turn the shower on and get in it. Make sure you wash all the shaving cream off your body. Each of you get a towel and dry off and then upstairs for pajamas. Got it?"

"Water fight!" Jamie yelled. Or maybe John. To be honest, she wasn't sure which.

She stepped up behind Ash. "If we catch you fighting in the shower, there will be no iPad time tomorrow."

There was an "Aw, man," and a reluctant "Yes, ma'am," but she figured they would forget within about a minute.

She glanced up at Ash. "One of us needs to—"

"Yeah, I'll check on them in a few. You get their pajamas?"

"Deal." Closing the bathroom door, Jordan called to Penny, who was in a heap on the floor at the base of the stairs. "I'm putting pajamas on your bed and setting the timer in your room. Teeth brushed and in the bed with a book by the time it goes off."

"I'm not ready to go to bed." Penny grumbled but grabbed her sleeping bag and stood up. Jordan caught her in a hug and gave her a kiss on the cheek. "I'll be up in a minute to tuck you in."

Screams came from the bathroom. Her eyes met Ash's over Levi's head. He passed Levi to her with a grin. "If I'm not out in five minutes, send help."

She was still chuckling as she climbed the stairs and changed Levi for bed. She would seriously have been in trouble had Ash not come to the rescue.

Tucking Levi under the Spiderman blanket, she leaned over to kiss his forehead. "I love you, Levi. I'll be back to check on you in a few minutes."

His eyes were already drooping when she stepped over the baby gate and into the hall and looked around to take stock. Penny was in the second-floor bathroom brushing her teeth.

With Ash right at their heels, the twins were tromping up the stairs, their towels around their waists. He pointed to their bedroom. "Get your jammies on and brush your teeth, please."

John—or Jamie—whipped his towel off his waist and snapped it at his brother, who ran squealing up the rest of the steps.

Ash came up the stairs after the twins, grabbed her and whispered in her ear. "There are way more of them than there are of us. First rule of parenting—don't let them see your fear."

Chapter Thirteen

Ash did his best to put on a serious face for the twins, but really, they were him and Joe at that age, to a T. "It's quiet time on the second floor. Remember, the little ones are going to sleep. No loud voices."

"I'll take them now if you want to tuck Penny in." Jordan followed the brothers to the door of their room, just down the hall.

"I've got Penny." He tucked the six-year-old into bed with her stuffed unicorn. "Night, sweet girl."

"Uncle Ash, will you pray with me?"

He hesitated, but knelt down by the little bed. "What do you want to pray about, my shiny Penny?"

Penny beamed at him and squeezed her big brown eyes closed tight. "Thank You for Mama Claire and Dad and Uncle Ash and Aunt J and my brothers and sisters and the dogs and the goats and the donkey and the horses. 'Specially Hagrid. Amen."

"Okay, sweetie—"

"I forgot the cats, Uncle Ash." Her little nose wrinkled up. "We can't forget the cats."

Ash took in a deep breath and said a small prayer

of his own, for patience. "And thank You, God, for the cats. Amen. Now, sleep tight, little bug."

He peeked into the twins' room. "Lights out, guys."

His breath was nearly knocked out of him as the twins rushed him, throwing their arms around his waist. They smelled like shaving cream and bubble gum. "Love you guys. Now sleep."

Jamie and John gave Jordan the same twin hug treatment, got rewarded with a kiss on the head, and scrambled into their beds, pulling the covers up. Ash recognized that it would be a small wonder if they stayed that way, but for now, they were all tucked in.

A quick peek into Amelia's room was his last stop. He tapped softly on the door, which was cracked. He could barely see Amelia's head sticking out of the covers, but he put a hand on his niece's forehead. Warm but not burning up. Jordan was waiting for him in the hall. "I think she's okay. Sleep is the best thing for now. The antibiotic will kick in tomorrow."

In the kitchen, Kiera handed Sweetness to Ash, who patted the littlest foster child on the back and made a raspberry at her when she grabbed his cheeks with her pudgy little hands. "She got tired of the high chair," Kiera said. "I changed her diaper, too."

"How's the studying going?" Jordan filled a bottle with water and measured the powder formula into it.

Collecting her computer and notecards into her backpack, Kiera rolled her eyes. "This teacher is so hard. There are like four hundred vocabulary words. I'm going to put the baby to bed and study some more. I'll see you tomorrow."

Jordan shook the bottle and handed it to Ash. "You okay with feeding Sweetness?"

"Sure." Ash sat on the sofa and slid the bottle into the baby's mouth, while Jordan collapsed on the sofa beside him.

"There are so many of them."

Ash laughed softly. "And they go in all directions, so you're always thinking you've lost one. You've got a little shaving cream…right there, on your cheek."

She rubbed it off and smirked. "You've got some, too, sport. Just there, above your right eyebrow."

Ash shook his head. "I don't even want to know."

He put Sweetness on his shoulder and patted her back.

"I'm gonna owe you big for this, aren't I?" Jordan asked.

"Yeah, I have something in mind. Hang on and let me put her in the crib and I'll be right back." He took Sweetness into Joe and Claire's bedroom, where the crib was pushed into a nook by the window.

Laying Sweetness gently on her back, he grabbed one of the half a dozen pacifiers in the crib and stuck it in her mouth before she could wake up.

Jordan had her feet on the coffee table and her eyes closed. When he came back into the living area, she cracked one blue-green eye. "I've only been here three hours. How can I be this tired in three hours?"

"I don't know. I feel it, though." He changed direction and went to the counter, where the single cup coffeemaker sat. He brewed two cups and brought the steaming mug to her on the couch. "It's a long time until they get home."

"Smart thinking."

Before he took a drink, he pulled out his personal diabetes manager and an alcohol pad. He swiped, pricked, watched the countdown, programmed the number into his PDM and put it away. He had a glucose monitor but still had to check his numbers the old-fashioned way a few times a day.

"So, the favor." Her eyes were all the way open now and on him, the mug cupped in her two hands.

"You remember I have a patient who's getting treated for cancer?"

"Rainbow fingernails."

He smiled. "Right. Rainbow fingernails. She's done with treatment, for now."

"She's, what do they call it, NED, no evidence of disease?"

"We won't know for sure until she has scans in another couple of weeks. This kid—Natalie—she loves horses. She knows all the different kinds and she's got pictures all over her room. I wondered if her mom could bring her out one day to meet the horses, maybe take a ride if she's up to it."

"That's not even a favor. I tell you what... My assistant and I have been working on an idea for children's parties. Why don't we try it out with her next weekend? She can bring her mom and dad and siblings, if she has 'em."

"The dad works offshore but we can ask. Jordan, I don't know how to thank you. This will be awesome."

"Tell her to wear a princess dress."

Natalie *was* a little princess and more than just a patient to him. He couldn't wait to see her face when they pulled up at the farm next week.

Upstairs, something crashed. His eyes locked with Jordan's. "I got this one."

* * *

"Get that banner up on the barn. We are T-minus ten minutes. No time for lollygagging around." Jordan's assistant, Allison, was on the job and they were counting down until Princess Natalie arrived for her party. Tablet in hand, Allison checked the banner off her ever-present digital list.

Jordan looked around, checking her own mental list. The picnic tables by the pond were decorated with sparkly gold crowns and yards and yards of pink tulle. Joe and Ash's sister Jules had done the food. Pale pink cupcakes with gold sprinkles, fruit kabob magic wands and perfectly frosted sugar cookies with tiny edible pearls at the tips. It was perfect.

The sky was crystal blue, one of those late-spring days when the humidity was low and there was a slight breeze, just enough to stir the leaves in the trees. It was almost enough to make up for the insanely hot weather to come. Almost.

A horn sounded on the highway and her pulse jumped. "They're here!"

Allison disappeared into the barn. Joe, the banner hanger, ran for his house and the cold six-pack of craft root beer she'd bribed him with.

Jordan straightened the burgundy velvet livery that Allison had unearthed from who-knew-where and gave Leo a rub on the neck. "Almost time, big man."

Her handsome horse, along with Bartlet and Hagrid, had been decked out with bows in their manes and tails and fancy velvet saddle blankets. The horses could sense the excitement, dancing a little as she and the volunteers held them.

She laughed out loud when the hot-pink Hummer

limo turned into the driveway. Ash had obviously pulled out all the stops for their princess of the day. The huge, gaudy car cruised to a stop and the door opened.

Ash stepped out first, tucked his crown under his arm and winked at her. The man had actually dressed like Prince Charming, in a white ceremonial uniform with miles of gold braid over red pants. If she'd thought she had a crush on him before, it was nothing compared to the rush of feelings she got when he held out his white-gloved hand and a tiny—also gloved—hand reached for his.

Their honorary princess was wearing a pink tulle dress with lots of bling and a crown on her sweet bald head. Jordan smiled. "Princess Natalie, welcome to Red Hill Castle.

"Your gallant steed is ready to take you to the royal picnic." Jordan turned to Leo and pressed the clicker in the palm of her hand while touching his shoulder. "Sir Leo, please honor our guest."

Leo stretched back and touched his nose to his lower leg in a deep bow, which had a huge smile stretching across the little girl's face.

"He's so pretty." Natalie had deep brown eyes that reminded her of Levi's, and they were glued to Leo. "Can I pet him?"

"Would you like to ride him?" Jordan kept a firm hand on Leo's lead rein and one hand on his neck. Fortunately, her oldest equine companion wasn't fazed by children dancing around him, and the volunteers who were working with her today were seasoned horse handlers.

Natalie's eyes searched for her mom, a petite woman

with a shiny black ponytail and tawny brown skin, who nodded at her daughter. "It's okay. You can ride him."

"You ready, Princess?" Ash stepped forward with a flourish of the hand.

"Ready, Doc—I mean, Prince Charming." Natalie giggled, and Ash's blue eyes met Jordan's. That carefree giggle from a five-year-old who hadn't that many reasons to laugh lately was worth all the work to set this day up.

Ash lifted Natalie onto Leo's back and handed her the reins.

"Look, Mommy, I'm so high! I'm a princess!"

"I see that, *mija*. You're a beautiful princess." Natalie's mom, with tears brimming in her eyes, walked a three hundred and sixty degree circle around her daughter, taking pictures.

"We're gonna take a slow turn around the 'castle courtyard' and then have the picnic by the pond." Jordan clucked to Leo and he started off at a very sedate pace, followed by the other horses carrying Natalie's siblings, who were also dressed for the occasion as a princess and a knight.

The whole party only lasted about half an hour, from beginning to end, including pony rides for Natalie and her siblings. The princess just didn't have the stamina for it. After the picnic, Ash carried her to the pink limo and tucked her into her booster seat.

Natalie's mom, circles under her own eyes, turned to Jordan, squeezing her in a hug. "I can't thank you enough for putting this together for Natalie. She's been through a lot—" she took a deep breath, settled "—and she really deserves a special day. Maybe a million of them."

"It was our pleasure. When she's feeling better, bring her back to the farm. It would be a way for her to regain strength that she would enjoy."

Carla nodded, dark eyes brightening. "She would love it." She stepped closer, glanced back toward the car. "So, it's none of my business, but I can see the way Doc looks at you. Don't let him get away. He's a keeper. We wouldn't have made it through this without him."

Jordan didn't respond and Carla didn't seem to care. At the limo, she grabbed Ash and whispered something in his ear, as well. Jordan could only guess.

He walked back to Jordan and held her hand as the limo drove down the driveway and out of sight. Together they turned and walked back to the picnic site. "Thank you for putting this together. It was amazing."

Jordan shook her head. "I really didn't have a lot to do with it. I just take orders well."

"Can I help you with the cleanup?"

"Actually, I'm leaving Allison in charge because Levi's caseworker is coming for her monthly visit and I need to go make sure all the plugs are covered and cabinet latches are where they're supposed to be. Later I'm taking my little man on an outing, though. Want to come?"

He looked down at his clothes. "Yeah, I should probably change first."

"Yeah, wear something casual. We're going to see Mr. Haney's new piglets."

"Aww, we're going to see my favorite food."

She threw her hat at him. "Go."

Jordan put Levi on the floor with some superlarge LEGO blocks. She was finding that he didn't stay put anymore; awesome for him, but a nightmare for her because he was into everything.

He wasn't pulling up yet but, little by little, he was getting stronger, thanks to his therapy—both traditional and equine therapy. She prayed every single day as Levi got stronger that he would be able to overcome the injury to his spine.

"Mama, wook!"

"Your tower looks great!" She would never tire of hearing that little voice. He'd been silenced for so long by abuse and neglect. He made her so proud, that he was working so hard to overcome all that he had been through. It was a tough kid that could come out the other side of that and still have the sweetest heart.

"Hey, buddy, what color is this one?"

Levi studied the big block she held. "Gween!"

"Good job. You're so smart!" She put a pot of coffee on. Reesa worked long hours, even sometimes on Saturday.

A quiet knock on the door and Reesa stuck her head in. "Hey, it's me."

"Come on in." She slid a plate of the practice cookies Jules had baked before the princess party onto the table.

"Are those cookies? I want one," Reesa said. "But first…"

The caseworker picked Levi up and swung him into the air, getting a belly laugh in return. "Little dude, you make my day."

She settled Levi on her hip and tickled his tummy when he grabbed one of her springy lavender curls. "Can he have a cookie?"

"Yes, if he wants one. He's still not a super-adventurous eater, but sometimes he surprises me." Levi took a piece of cookie from Reesa. "Like now."

Reesa put Levi back on the quilt on the floor and accepted the mug of coffee that Jordan poured. "Speaking of surprises, you should probably sit down for this one. I had a visit with Levi's mom a few days ago."

"You went to see her in jail?"

"Yes. She called and left a message that she wanted to talk, so I arranged a visit. She told me that she's thought about it and she would like to relinquish her parental rights."

Jordan's chest felt like it had a vise around it. She forced in a breath. "You mean, like, for good?"

"Yes, that's what that means. I'm not sure of her motivation. She's going to be in prison for a good stretch, so that may be it. Maybe she's pregnant again and doesn't want a termination to affect her rights to future kids. I just don't know."

"When would this happen?"

"It won't be overnight. The paperwork has to be done and then we'll have to get a court date. And I don't know about the father. I'm going to talk to him, too, and see if we can get permanency for this little guy. He deserves that."

"Yes, he does." Jordan looked over to the floor, where Levi was playing with some magazines he'd pulled down from the coffee table. He grinned at her.

How many tears had she shed over his situation since he got here? More than she could count, she knew. She'd never been face-first on the floor praying so hard for anything as she had prayed for Levi—for his health and for his happiness, for stability in whatever form it came.

Reesa's voice was gentle as it broke through her thoughts. "No promises, Jordan, but you're his foster mom, so our preference would be that he stay with you since there are no relatives willing to step in. Will you think about adoption and let me know if that's something you would be willing to do?"

She nodded, the knot of feelings in her throat too big to speak around.

Reesa patted her hand and stood up, folding the cover over her notepad. "Okay, good. Now, I need to go before I eat another cookie. Man, those are good."

Jordan walked her to the door. "Thank you, Reesa. I know one thing. Levi is lucky to have you on his team."

Reesa laughed. "No doubt."

The caseworker hitched her big leather bag over her shoulder and started around the pond, tiptoeing so her high-heeled shoes didn't sink into the grass.

Jordan shut the door, her mind reeling. She'd thought about adoption, had said as much to Ash. She hadn't let her mind really go there, though. Maybe it was some form of self-preservation, telling herself that if he had to go she would be okay with it.

Now she was in a position where she had to think about it, had to think about whether being a part of her family would be what was best for Levi.

"Mama, wook!" She probably heard those words a hundred times a day now. And at least fifty of them, she corrected him. Mama J.

What would it be like to actually be Levi's mama?

This thought seemed premature in a lot of ways, but

what about Ash? If their relationship continued to progress, how would he feel about being an instant parent?

It was a lot to think about.

And they had to go see some little pigs.

Chapter Fourteen

Mr. Haney, in his signature overalls, greeted them at the car with a smile lighting up his kind gray eyes. Ash had a special place in his heart for Mr. Haney, ever since he was a kid. Mr. H had come to visit him once a week when he was sick, bringing a loaf of fresh-baked bread from Mrs. H and farm fresh butter.

Often, in those days, Mr. Haney would show up on Ash's doorstep with a kitten or a puppy or a boxful of chicks. Anything to take a young boy's mind off cancer. There was nothing sophisticated about Harvey Haney, but there was an easy acceptance and that had meant the world to a sick little boy.

"Well, if it ain't the town doctor. Haven't seen you in a while. You been busy with this measles outbreak, I guess."

"Yes, sir." Ash unbuckled Levi and picked him up from his car seat. "It's starting to wind down now."

"Nothing new in the world, is there? I remember being a child and the measles breaking out. Polio, too. Always in the summer months. My mother wouldn't let us out of her sight. Had to swim in our old lukewarm pond instead of going to the creek like everyone else."

Ash nodded. "My grandmother would talk about that. It was a scary time."

Jordan hugged Mr. Haney as she came around the car. "We've been so excited about coming to see the piglets and our favorite farmer."

"Now then, we're glad that Levi could come out and see Pappy's new pigs." Mr. Haney held out his hands and Levi dove into the old man's arms. "Mary Pat's got some lemonade on the patio for you two grown-ups. Levi and Pappy are going for a little walk."

Ash smiled, watching the three-year-old bounce in Mr. Haney's arms as they walked away, knowing from experience that Mr. Haney would talk to Levi about the cows and pigs and plants on the farm, patiently telling him the names of each one.

As Ash and Jordan walked around to the backyard, they were greeted by an enthusiastic cocker spaniel.

Mr. Haney's daughter Mary Pat, a blonde with a heart of gold, bustled toward them. "Bristow, get down. I swear that dog would jump up and lick your face if he could. Ash, are things settling down for you at all?"

"Yes, thanks. We haven't had any new cases of measles in the last week, so hopefully we're getting close to being in the clear. How's my prom date doing?" He wrapped his arms around the youngest Haney daughter. He and M.P. had dated for about five minutes their junior year before they both realized that being friends was a lot more fun.

"Life is good. Helping out around the farm is keeping me and the kids busy. We can't keep up with Dad, though, now that he's back on his feet." She smiled, and now when she did, there was a light in her eyes. When she'd first moved back to Red Hill Springs to care for her ailing father, she'd just been through a divorce and her eyes were decidedly world-weary.

"No one could ever keep up with Mr. H." Ash grinned and lounged in one of the deck chairs, Jordan settling beside him.

"No, and we have the piglets in the barn and new puppies in the laundry room. Bristow here is a proud daddy—okay, more like a confused, indifferent daddy, but still. The puppies are cute."

Jordan glanced toward the barn where Mr. Haney had disappeared with Levi.

"He'll be fine," M.P. said. "Daddy's been hauling kids all over this land for years. He has a knack."

"I've seen it in action." Jordan sat in the chair across the table from Ash. Mary Pat put a frosty glass of lemonade and a small plate of banana bread in front of each of them.

Ash picked his glass up and drank with a long, smooth gulp. He reached for Jordan's hand. "Levi's fine. He's over being sick and he's doing great."

Jordan squeezed his fingers. "I know. I never thought I'd be one of those moms, but when he got so sick, I don't know. It just happened."

M.P. looked between their hands and Ash's face. His cheeks got warm, but he didn't let go of Jordan's hand, tossing a piece of banana bread back with his other hand.

She caught Ash's gaze with a raised eyebrow. "I know how that is. Ross crashed his bike and broke his elbow last summer. I was paranoid for months."

Ash took another drink of lemonade. He was so

thirsty. The weather was unusually hot, or at least it seemed that way. Was it his blood sugar? He should probably test.

Jordan glanced up at him and back at Mary Pat. "When do you start your clinicals?"

"I finish my course work as soon as I take finals and I'll start at the hospital the next week. I can't wait. It's taken me forever to finish school."

"I know your kids will be so proud of you. And your dad."

M.P. smiled. "Yeah, and I'll feel better once I'm contributing to the household finances. It's been hard—I feel like I'm always *taking*, even though it is from my own family."

"I felt that way when I moved here after Claire. She was all established and had made friends. It just takes some time, I think. This banana bread is delicious, Mary Pat."

Ash leaned his head back against the chair. He was so sleepy sitting in the sun. He could hear the hum of conversation from the women and just let himself drift.

Jordan shook his shoulder. Her voice sounded as if it came from a long way away. "Ash! Wake up!"

He opened his eyes and tried to focus on her face. She was blurry and his fuzzy brain realized that he was hyperglycemic. "I need to test."

Digging his PDM out of his pocket, he roused himself enough to prick his finger. His blood glucose level was three-twenty after having banana bread and lemonade. *Duh*. No wonder he felt so sick and sleepy. He forced himself to focus on the screen, programming a bolus of insulin with clumsy fingers. His tongue felt thick in his mouth.

Jordan stayed at his side, talking to him, making jokes, anything to keep him awake. He heard the lower rumble of Mr. Haney's voice, but kept his eyes on Jordan's. His average blue to her brilliant. They weren't even *just* blue. Bright blue around deep green with brown flecks.

He smiled at her. She was really so pretty. He would kiss her if he didn't feel so lousy.

His thoughts sharpened and he realized his fast-acting insulin was kicking in. He'd nearly made a very serious mistake, one he hadn't made in a long time, because he'd let himself get distracted. It happened—part of life as a diabetic—but forgetting for a minute that he had a life-threatening disease could very literally threaten his life, and he was usually more careful.

He sat up in the chair and drank from the glass of water Mary Pat pushed into his hands. "I'm fine, guys. Thanks."

Concern still lingered in Jordan's eyes. "Do you want to go?"

Mr. Haney held a hand out to Ash, hauling him to his feet, and looking him over. "You're looking a bit peaky, yet."

"No. I'm good now. I promise," he said to the still skeptical Jordan. "Besides, we haven't seen the piglets, yet."

Mr. Haney clapped his hands together. "Let's go, then. We're bottle-feeding this lot since the sow refused to nurse them. It's gonna get messy."

Jordan watched Ash as they played with the little pigs. He did seem to be fine, if still a little pale.

He held a little pink pig with brown spots and fed it

a bottle. The baby dribbled more than he drank. Luckily, M.P. kept a load of old towels washed and in the barn for this purpose. Jordan handed one to Ash, who tucked it under the piglet's neck, like he would a baby.

The tiny pigs were no bigger than the length of her arm and were the cutest things she had ever seen, especially the way they played with Levi. One little guy in particular would trot up to the toddler, who was sitting cross-legged next to Jordan, put his teeny hooves on Levi's chest and sniff his face. Levi would belly laugh, the piglet would run back to his sisters and brothers and the whole thing would start over again.

"I believe that little pig needs a new home at Red Hill Farm." Mr. Haney's deep chuckle tickled Jordan.

She laughed. "It's tempting, but I think we have enough of a menagerie as it is. The goats alone are about to make me lose my hair."

"All right, then. You put those little 'uns back in their stall when they're finished eating. I'm gonna take Levi down to the pond and feed the fish. No getting bored around here, young man. There's always something that needs doing." Mr. Haney stood and held his hands out to Levi, who immediately reached for his new best buddy.

"Yes, sir, I know how it is." Jordan picked up another piglet, this one solid black. It squealed and she almost dropped it, but she stuck the bottle in its mouth and it eagerly attacked the food. The barn was dim, dust swirling in the light streaming through cracks and crevices in the old building.

This barn, like her own, smelled like fresh hay, animals and a hint of freshly oiled leather.

Ash had a damp washcloth that Mr. Haney had used

to wipe the piglets off after they ate and he was gently cleaning up the pigs they had just fed. He glanced up to catch her watching him and sighed.

"I'm sorry about before," he said softly.

"What? No, it's fine. I mean, not fine because I'm sorry it happened, but I'm not freaked out or anything. Maybe worried, a little, that it might happen to you when no one is around."

He didn't look at her and she worried that she'd said the wrong thing, but then he met her eyes, seeking her understanding. "I have good control using the continuous glucose monitor and insulin pump, but there are times that everything goes wrong. Sometimes the insulin pump isn't placed right or my body is just particularly resistant to the insulin. There's nothing I can do about that. But usually if there's a problem, it's because of user error. Today I forgot to program a bolus of insulin before eating Mary Pat's banana bread and drinking lemonade."

He shrugged, frustration evident on his face. "I guess I get to feeling like a normal person who does normal person things and I don't want to stop to be a diabetic again, even though I know I have to do things a certain way."

"I can understand that." She took the washcloth out of his hand and wiped the chin of the black piglet.

"It wasn't a conscious decision, but I'll be more careful. I really am sorry."

She released the piglet she was holding into the stall Mr. Haney had prepared for them and sat down on the barn floor face-to-face with Ash, their knees touching. "You don't have to explain to me unless you want to. I know you have the pump and the monitor and I'm grateful to them for helping keep you alive, so that I can know what an incredible person you are. I don't care—at all—that you're a diabetic. I just want you to be safe."

He took a deep breath, his shoulders relaxing a little bit. "Okay. If you say so."

She leaned forward, pressing a kiss to his lips, laughing at his surprised expression. "Stop worrying. If you're good, I'm good. Come on, let's go. I want to take pictures of Levi down by the pond."

She followed him out of the barn and tried to ignore the way her heart filled up with happiness when his hand slid into hers.

Ash lifted a very sleepy Levi from his car seat. "I've never seen a nonmobile kid get this dirty."

"Might've had something to do with the fact that Mr. Haney let him play with a bucket full of fishing worms." She slung the diaper bag over her shoulder. "Not enough wipes in the world for that."

With Levi on his hip, Ash followed Jordan around the pond, falling into step beside her. "If you're wondering what that sound is, my shoes are squishing."

"I told you not to dress up."

He spread his free hand and looked at her like she was crazy. "My shirt's untucked?"

She laughed. "Yeah, wow. I don't know how I missed that obvious sign."

"This is the third pair of shoes I've ruined this month."

She tried not to laugh; he could tell by the way the dimple deepened in the corner of her mouth. In the end, though, she couldn't keep the laugh from slipping out.

He entertained Levi as Jordan gave the dirty tod-

dler a quick bath in her farmhouse sink and dressed
him in soft short pajamas.

She lifted Levi into her arms. "Want to go sit outside? It's too nice a night for us to be cooped up inside."

When Ash nodded, she grabbed a quilt from a rack
by the door and laid it in the grass by the pond. Levi
had a little second wind from his bath but played quietly with his cars beside them on the quilt.

Claire and Joe's younger kids were on the play set in
their backyard, and the sound of kids laughing and playing carried in the soft evening air. It was peaceful—the
pond reflecting the sky, the animals blowing and shuffling—one of those summer nights that just seemed to
stretch. Ash took a deep breath, just because he could.

"Hey, look," Jordan whispered.

When Ash glanced over, Levi's eyes were dipping
closed. He smiled. "Piglets and worms wear a guy out.
Hey, I forgot to ask how things went with the caseworker?"

"It was good. I always get nervous, but it was fine."
She paused. "Reesa said that Levi's mother talked to
her about relinquishing her parental rights."

"Wow. That's quite a development."

"Yeah, it really is. I'm trying not to get my hopes
up." She didn't look at him, but he could see the tension in her face.

"What are you thinking?"

She stared across the pond, her voice almost a whisper. "I don't want him to ever feel unwanted or unloved.
It kills me to think about him going to someone else
after everything he's been through. I just don't know if
I'm the best person to give him what he needs."

"Jordan, I'm a cancer survivor and an insulin-dependent diabetic. You saw what happened today. I'm the definition of relationship risk. Watching you be a mother to Levi has shown me that the best attribute for a relationship is not perfection, it's love. And, babe, you've got the love part down."

She looked away and for a long minute he was afraid he'd said something wrong, until she turned around, scrubbing tears off her face. She flipped onto her stomach so her face was even with his. He reached up and tucked a piece of hair behind her ear, taking the opportunity to slide his fingers down her cheek.

When her eyes widened, Ash leaned closer, letting his lips hover over hers.

"Why do you second-guess yourself?" he murmured. "You amaze me every single day, Jordan. The way your mind works, the way your heart is always big enough for whatever comes your way."

Her lips trembled and he caught them in a kiss.

"It's probably a good thing we have an audience. You make me feel things that I never imagined I would, Jordan." Ash paused. "You make me feel brave, like I can do anything."

"You can."

"You can, too." He locked his gaze with hers. "I love you, Jordan."

The words came of their own volition, out of the feelings she stirred in him. He was so close he could hear her breath quicken. Tears slid down her cheeks again and he rubbed them away with his thumb.

She cupped his cheek with her hand and let her lips roam over his face, the tender kisses nearly undoing him.

Her gaze met his, the vulnerability still in her eyes.

"I need to get Levi in bed. Tomorrow is Sunday and it's always crazy. Will you be here for Sunday lunch?"

"Unless something comes up. I'm on call this weekend."

"Okay. Monday we start prepping for the horse show. My clients are so excited to show off their skills for their parents and friends."

"I gotta head home, too." Ash got to his feet and held his hand out for her. She slid her fingers into his and he lifted her to her feet, wondering if maybe he had spoken too soon.

He held her hand in both of his. Strong and sturdy, nails clipped short, her hands were working hands. He loved them; he loved her.

And really, he just wondered why it had taken him so long to realize it.

Chapter Fifteen

Jordan stood in the back of the church with Levi on her hip. He wasn't super-pumped about being in the service, but when she'd tried to put him in the nursery, he'd had an epic meltdown.

The nursery worker had given her a disbelieving look when she'd pulled him close and said they would try again next week. The children's minister had patted Levi on the back and told Jordan that all kids went through separation anxiety.

Jordan had held her tongue when what she wanted to do was haughtily inform the children's minister that all children hadn't suffered severe trauma and abuse and some of them needed time, sometimes a lot of time, to learn that their caregiver could be trusted.

She rubbed Levi's little back as she swayed. He was finally relaxing the death grip he'd had on her neck. She sighed. It wasn't the nursery worker's fault and it wasn't the children's minister's fault. For most people, the idea of a child being genuinely afraid his caregiver wouldn't come back for him wasn't a real thing. In Levi's world, it was. And so, Jordan held her tongue and stood between him and the world that was so anxious for him to grow up and act normal.

When he pointed at Claire, who was sitting on the other side of the church, and said, "Wook, Mama," Jordan slid out the double doors and into the parking lot. Thirty seconds later Penny came out right behind her.

"Mama Claire said I could come outside with you."

Jordan tugged on one of Penny's braids, just like her own, except Penny's were blond. "Of course you can, pumpkin. Want to play on the playground? Maybe they have a swing that Levi can swing in."

The door slammed open behind her and one of the twins blew through it. "I'm coming, too."

Penny ran ahead and, in characteristic Penny fashion, was through the fence and at the top of the slide before Jordan could even get out of the parking lot, John right behind her.

As she walked, Levi laid his head on her shoulder, his little body getting heavy. "Hey, guys, I'm gonna stay over here in the shade. Levi's getting sleepy."

Jordan stood under the entrance overhang of the children's wing, watching the kids slide and swing. As much as they'd been through, they were resilient, laughing and playing.

The door swung out beside her, hiding her from view. She started to step out, so she could say hello, until she heard a snippet of what they were saying.

"The horsey one, what's her name? She wouldn't put that little boy in the nursery. He's three years old. Or so she says."

Jordan froze. She, apparently, was the *horsey one*.

"I don't know, Lou Ellen." The second voice was hesitant. "She seems okay."

The first voice again, the tone lower. "And that kindergartener, honestly, her language is so vulgar."

Jordan heard footsteps and then, "Hey, Shiny Penny."

Ash.

"Doc! Hey, Doc! Watch me slide. I can go really fast, like I'm sliding from the moon!"

Ash chuckled. "Good one!"

One of the women called from the doorway, "Oh, Dr. Sheehan, I see you're running late. Did you have an emergency this morning?"

Ash looked toward the door and caught her eye, the expression on his face somewhere between curiosity and annoyance. She held her finger to her lips, imploring him not to reveal that she was standing there.

The women would know that she had overheard the whole thing.

"Are those kids on the playground by themselves? I think I'm going to have to bring that up at the next church council meeting. Children shouldn't be allowed out here unaccompanied."

"Oh, no worries, Lou Ellen, I'm watching them." Ash leaned on the fence, his dimples deepening as he smiled.

The second voice, the one Jordan didn't recognize, spoke again. "That's fine, Ash. I'm sure they're in good hands."

"I don't understand where her mother, I mean, foster mother, is." Lou Ellen sniffed. "It's a shame you're having to miss the service, Dr. Sheehan."

"Oh, that's okay. Jordan and I were just out here enjoying the breeze while the children play." Ash's shoulders shook with suppressed laughter.

Jordan's eyes went wide. Her cheeks were flaming as she clapped a hand over her mouth.

"Well, I suppose that's... *Jordan?*" Lou Ellen's voice sounded strangled.

Jordan stepped out from behind the door and nodded. "Ladies."

Her head held high, she crossed to stand by Ash's side. He put his arm around her, pulling her close with a smile for the women in the open door. "You were saying?"

With a little bit of spluttering from Lou Ellen, and bright spots of color on the cheeks of the other woman, they excused themselves to go back to their Sunday School classes.

Ash held Jordan's arm as they walked into the playground area where there was a picnic table. "So, I got the idea that they were talking about you and you overheard?"

"It's just been a morning. The nursery people don't like it that I won't leave Levi when he cries. The children's minister thinks it's only separation anxiety and every kid has it. I was already feeling a little beat up and then those two came out. The kids couldn't hear them or I would have stepped in to say something."

"So, you stood there listening while they ran you down? I'm so sorry." He squeezed her hand and looked up as Penny called his name again. "I'm watching, sweet girl."

Jordan shrugged. "They just don't understand. It's okay."

"Most people absolutely love the kids at Red Hill Farm. They're so happy that they get to know the kids and serve them in small ways through our church." He made a noise of dismissal. "Lou Ellen has always been that way. She was downright mean to Joe when he was little, but she was the first one to stand in the receiving line when he became chief of police. Everyone knows how she is. People won't listen to her."

"Thank you. That makes me feel better, but you always do seem to know what to say." She tilted her head. "I hear the organ music starting. I guess that means the service is almost over."

"Oh, good, that means we get lunch now. You're going to be at the farm?"

Jordan eased to her feet, trying not to wake Levi. Clouds were gathering overhead, white piled on gray piled on steel. "Of course. Claire would kill me if I missed Sunday lunch. It looks like we might be inside, though. You?"

"I'm on call, but so far so good." He grinned as he stood. "But I don't want to experience the wrath of Claire, either."

The front doors of the church opened and people poured out, the other twin, Jamie, stopping to high-five Pastor Rick, who laughed and shook his head.

John ran toward his brother, and Ash snaked a long arm and snagged him by the back of the shirt. "Oh, no, you don't." To Jordan, he said, "Joe's not here, so I'll help Claire round up the hooligans. You should go. It looks like the bottom is going to fall out any minute."

"I'm headed that way. I'll take Penny with me."

She started toward the swings, wind whipping her hair.

"Jordan."

When she turned around, his blue eyes were intense on hers. "Be careful."

The simple words echoed through her heart. "I will. You be careful, too. Hey, Penny, let's go, kiddo."

The little girl skipped over from the swings and slid her soft little hand in Jordan's. Penny's eyes were shining, her confidence a tender shoot to be nurtured into blooming. Jordan swung their hands between them, smile widening at Penny's unrestrained laughter when the wind blew her dress.

It didn't matter what anyone else said. Their kids were a gift, every single one of them.

Sheets of rain slammed the antebellum home that housed Claire and Joe's ever-growing family. A little rain wasn't going to stop Sunday lunch from happening, though. Joe was outside on the porch, grilling hot dogs. Jordan, with Levi in the carrier on her back, finished a huge bowl of potato salad with some chopped chives and set it on the island, dodging little kids playing chase through the bar stools. She glanced around the room, wondering where Ash was. Maybe an emergency had come up that he had to deal with.

Joe and Ash's sister Jules set a tray of peanut butter sandwiches, always a hit with the kids, beside Jordan's salad. "I don't know how Claire doesn't lose her mind. The noise level alone would send me over the edge."

Jordan smiled. "I think she's used to it. Either that or she's lost her hearing."

"Definitely lost her hearing. Wow."

Oldest foster child Kiera's sister Shauna set a couple of bags of chips on the island. "Of course my two boys increase the decibels by at least ten."

"How's school? Is your semester almost over?" Jordan asked. Shauna had aged out of foster care three years earlier and, against all odds, was working her way through college with two kids.

"Yes. I sent in my application for nursing school so I'll hear something in a month or so. I'm so scared."

"You've got the grades and you've worked really hard to have some experience going in. Where's your mom today?"

A sad look crossed Shauna's face. "I haven't seen her in a couple of weeks. She sent me one text that said she was going to rehab again, but in Tonya-speak, that means she's probably going to score and who knows when she'll surface."

Jordan put a hand on Shauna's arm. "I'm sorry."

Shauna shrugged. "Hey, we survive, right? I'm fine. Kiera's getting it together and she has Claire and you for role models."

"And you. She has a big sister who's a great role model."

Joe came into the kitchen with a huge tray of hot dogs and set it on the island with the rest of the food. "Hey, everyone, hit the ballroom. It's time to pray."

In the hall, he gave a shrill whistle with his thumb and fingers in his mouth and kids came from everywhere, spilling out into the common area. "Ballroom for prayers before the hot dogs get cold."

Their circle stretched halfway around the ballroom and they were beginning to look a little like the United Nations, but when they held hands and prayed, none of that mattered. They were a family—the weirdest family ever, but family nonetheless. And for Jordan, who grew up with just a sister and a mom, this big, loving, fighting, singing, playing, very imperfect family was absolutely perfect for her.

She looked around the circle for Ash but didn't see him. After the crowd dispersed for the kitchen, she grabbed Joe's elbow. "Hey, have you heard from Ash?"

Joe jerked his thumb toward the porch. "He's got Penny's little brother, Josiah. The caseworker brought him last night. I stayed home with him this morning."

"Oh, okay, thanks!" She turned toward the door and then looked back at Joe. "Wait—I thought it was an older brother."

Joe grinned. "Yeah, so did we. How about I take Levi and get him a hot dog?"

"Sure." She turned her back to her brother-in-law and he plucked his foster nephew out of the carrier.

"Come on, dude, let's go get some food."

Jordan slid out of the carrier and out the front door. No one even noticed. They were too busy loading their plates in the kitchen.

The storm had let up, for the moment, but the rain was still coming down. The air had a cool crispness to it, as if it had just been washed and shaken out to dry. The porch, like the yard, was dim, but Ash sat at the far end, in the porch swing, with a tow-headed little boy about four years old.

Ash had his head leaned back against the swing, his eyes closed, and he was gently rocking the swing with his big toe. Her heart did that thing where it felt like it was melting in her chest. He'd had her so convinced that he was a card-carrying member of the Girl-of-the-Month club. He didn't look like that guy this afternoon.

She must've made a noise because he opened his eyes and the corner of his mouth lifted in a sleepy half smile. "Hey."

The little boy's arms tightened around Ash's neck.

"Josiah's a little anxious with so many people around, so we're just hanging out."

"You need something to eat. Why don't I take him for a little while?"

"I'm good right now. I had a snack before I got to church. Where's Levi?"

"Joe snuck him out of the backpack and took him in for a manly hot dog."

"So, not a regular dog, a manly one." Ash grinned and slowed down his rocking so she could ease onto the swing with him. "Any word from Reesa today?"

"Nothing. It's probably going to take some time for her to set up a visit with the dad." She rolled her shoulders, aware her easy words didn't exactly reflect her tension-knotted muscles.

"I'm sorry. It's so hard waiting. And even harder to trust that it will all work out the way it is supposed to." The little boy, Josiah, squirmed in Ash's arms. He opened his eyes, scowled at Jordan, made an unhappy noise and squinched his eyes closed again.

The door flew open and Claire stepped out on the porch. "Oh, there he is. I thought I lost him. There are so many people around and so many hiding places in this house. Come on, Josiah. Time to eat. Penny's waiting for you inside."

Josiah opened his eyes and put his hand in Claire's, sliding off Ash's lap to the floor. At the door, Claire looked back. "Come on, guys. Coast is just about clear, but the boys will be back for seconds any minute. Now's your chance."

The door slammed behind her and Jordan laughed. "She's always been bossy like that."

Ash's phone buzzed in his pocket and he pulled it

out. She wondered what kind of emergency call he would be answering.

He looked up from his phone and said, "It's Latham, my friend who's contracting the work on the river house for me. Some shingles blew off the roof. We've got to put a tarp on it or the new floors are going to be ruined." He glanced up at her, regret in his eyes. "I'm sorry."

"I'll come with you."

"No, you stay with Levi. I'll see you later." His long fingers cupped her cheek and he pressed a kiss to her lips with a grin. "I still love you."

Before she could gather her thoughts to answer, he was down the steps and into his car. She watched his red taillights until he turned onto the highway, her fingers on her lips.

He was right. It was hard to wait. Hard to trust. She wanted to trust Ash. Wanted to trust that *I love you's* meant he was in it for the long haul.

She was close, looking over the cliff at the big, blue water down below. She wanted to run for the edge, not a thought in her head except what the wind would feel like in her hair as she flew.

But she wondered, was it a risk that she could take if she was risking more than just her own heart?

The deluge was over by the time Ash pulled up at the construction site for his house, replaced by a soft downpour that had him drenched to the skin in seconds as he ran for the covered front porch. Latham was waiting, kicked back in a folding chair.

"I put some buckets out in the house. We'll have to wait out the rain to put the tarp up. Otherwise, the roof'll try to kill you." Latham's drawl was low and slow. In fact, there wasn't much about Latham that wasn't deliberate, which Ash guessed was what made him a good contractor.

He and Ash had played soccer together in high school, as well as their more recent pickup games. Latham had played goalie, his big legs and muscular arms making him a perfect wall of defense.

Ash opened the door to the house and got a couple of cold drinks out of the cooler in the kitchen. He tossed one to Latham and sat in the other folding chair, propping his feet on the rail. The river was a gray blur, just a slight shade difference from the water to the woods beyond.

"So that woman you're seeing, the one who was out here the other day. Y'all got a thing going on?" Latham pulled a little piece of wood out of one of the many pockets in his cargo pants and started whittling at it.

"Yeah, something like that."

"Thinking of a future with that little boy, too?"

"Yes, the little boy, too. His name is Levi."

Latham nodded, his dark eyes narrowed on the non-existent view. "I guess if that little one can't walk, we'll be needing to do some adjustments on the bathroom shower. The porch will be needing a ramp, too."

Ash startled, shooting a look at Latham. He hadn't thought at all about including Jordan as he renovated the house, hadn't thought about Levi being here and what that would mean. Hadn't realized until just that minute how much he wanted Levi to stay.

"What about you? Ever think about getting married again?" Ash shot a look at Latham, who was shaking his head.

"Nope. These days I'm more interested in a good steak and a cold drink. Unless your mama's available. I've always been kinda sweet on Bertie." Latham grinned, his tanned face creasing with laughter.

Ash laughed. "You and half the town."

Rain had slowed to a drizzle when Latham put his pocket knife away. "You ready to get this beast installed? I figure we have about a half an hour before the next squall hits."

Latham stuck the blue tarp under his arm and was up the ladder in about two seconds. He walked the roof just like he was on the ground. "Hand me one of those one-by-ones, will ya?"

With Ash handing supplies up to the roof and Latham working, the tarp was screwed down in less than thirty minutes. Latham came back down the ladder as the first fat drops fell from the sky.

The contractor put his drill carefully away in one of the lockboxes in the back of his pickup and slammed it shut. "I'll text you and let you know when I'll be working this week. I should be finishing up that deck over at the Marshalls' house by Tuesday."

"Sounds good. Thanks, man."

With a roar of the huge engine, Latham started down the gravel drive that led to the highway, leaving Ash to walk around the house, as he often did.

He opened the front door and stepped into the great room. Latham had knocked down a wall between the front room and the kitchen and installed an island between the two. The fireplace would go there with new stone around it.

In his mind, he saw Jordan with her feet up to the fire, in the winter.

He closed his eyes. For the island in the kitchen he'd gone with smooth marble, and the countertops were going to be a light-colored butcher block. He'd thought when he picked it out that maybe he would learn to cook.

It wasn't some low-blood-sugar-induced hallucination when, in his mind, he saw Jordan at the sink, laughing as she watched Levi playing outside. When did it happen that he stopped imagining himself growing old alone?

He'd never thought that he would fall in love, get married, do all the things that people normally imagine they will do. But Jordan didn't see him as a disease, any more than she saw her young clients as their disability.

In some weird way, she had chosen him, seen something in him that most people didn't bother to look for—the tender part of him that he liked to pretend wasn't there.

She seemed to think that she was the only one risking her heart. Did she not realize his heart was every bit as much in her hands as hers was in his?

Chapter Sixteen

A week later Jordan plopped into the red vinyl booth at the Hilltop Café across from Levi's caseworker. "I'm exhausted. Our first annual horse show is in two weeks and I'm losing my mind. My to-do list is about seven miles long."

Ash's mom, Bertie, slid a mug of coffee onto the table in front of Jordan. "Blueberry pancakes?"

"Yes, ma'am. Reesa?" Meeting for breakfast had been the caseworker's idea, and the tiny part of Jordan's mind that wasn't occupied with her to-do list was dying for information.

"Just coffee in a to-go cup, please." Reesa looked down at her phone as she dashed out a text before setting it down on the table again.

Jordan raised one eyebrow. "You're going to regret not ordering food and let me just say that when you do, you will have to get your own pancakes."

Reesa laughed, checking her phone again as it buzzed. "I wish I had time for pancakes. I have another appointment in a few minutes."

A waitress came by with a to-go cup and filled it

with coffee for Reesa, leaving a few small containers of half-and-half on the table.

The caseworker opened the half-and-half, poured it into her coffee and took a sip. "Oh, that's better. Okay, are you ready for some good news? Both biological parents have signed forms to relinquish their parental rights, so if you want to adopt Levi, it can probably be done within about eight weeks."

Jordan couldn't speak. Her heart in her throat was about to choke her. So many feelings. Relief mingled with grief for the loss Levi suffered, almost instantly followed by the fear that she wasn't…enough. Good enough, strong enough, wise enough, to be Levi's mother.

On the table, Reesa's phone buzzed again. She looked at the readout and sighed. "I've got to go. One of my teenagers is in crisis and it looks like we're going to have to get her into a residential treatment program today."

Reesa snapped the lid onto her coffee cup and slid closer to the edge of her seat. "Think about what you want to do and let me know by Friday. We have families who are adopt-only, but we'd want to move Levi as soon as possible if that's the way we're going to go."

She slid out of the booth, her phone already buzzing in her hand again. "I'll touch base with you soon."

The idea of them moving Levi made Jordan physically sick, so much so that when Bertie placed the plate of pancakes in front of her, still steaming from the griddle, she knew she couldn't eat them.

Bertie slid into the spot Reesa had just vacated, setting down her coffeepot on the table. "Jordan, honey, what's going on? All the color drained from your face."

"Reesa is Levi's caseworker. She asked me if I'd

consider adopting him. Both of his biological parents surrendered their rights."

"That's wonderful!" Bertie stopped and studied Jordan's face again. "Right?"

"It is. I mean, it will be so great for him to have a permanent home and family. I just hope I'm the right person to give him the stability he needs."

She'd gone into being a foster parent with blinders on, with a heart full of love for kids who needed it and a desire to change the world for the better. She knew it would hurt and it would be hard, but she could handle it.

She'd almost had herself convinced, but each time one of the kids left Red Hill Farm, they took a part of her heart with them.

Jordan knew that if she chose to adopt Levi, she couldn't go into adoption with blinders on. Adoption was forever. For her and for Levi it was a decision that couldn't be undone. She couldn't raise the white flag when she reached the end of her abilities.

"What's the alternative if you decide not to adopt?" Bertie's voice was calm and she asked a reasonable question that made Jordan's heart quake in her chest.

"They would move him to an adoptive home as soon as possible." Tears formed in her eyes as she said the words.

"Oh, honey. What worries you about adopting Levi? What's giving you second thoughts?"

"I'd be a single mom to a child with multiple special needs, some that we don't even know about right now." Her throat clamped down on the words. "What if I can't do it?"

"I have some experience at having a child with special needs. There's no love like the love of a mother for her child and when your child is sick, it requires more of you than anything you can imagine, but every day, it's worth it. There's no greater joy than seeing your child thrive and succeed despite the obstacles they face."

"You're talking about Ash."

Bertie's blue eyes, so much like her son's, searched Jordan's face. "Yes. He told you?"

"Yes. He's— We've— He's really special to me, Bertie." She swallowed hard over what seemed like a permanent lump in her throat. "When I make the decision to adopt, I'm not just making the decision for me. It's a decision that affects my whole family and...everyone in my life."

"Including Ash?"

"Yes, I think so. I hope so. Oh, Bertie, I don't know."

Bertie put her hand over Jordan's and squeezed. "Being with Ash through all the health issues he had was one of the greatest honors of my life. It's scary and it's sad and it's heartbreaking, but I wouldn't trade being his mother for anything under the sun."

"I love Levi that much." She remembered Ash's words to her that relationships are not about perfection, they're about love.

"I can see that. You love him enough that you're willing to let him go if you think that's the best thing for him. That sounds like a mother's love to me, Jordan."

Bertie got out of the booth and came around to her side, wrapping her arms around Jordan. "Sweet Jordan, you don't have to worry. There's enough love in your heart to do whatever you want to do."

"Thanks, Bertie." She left money on the table for her meal, grabbed her bag and left. When she got outside, she stood on the sidewalk for a minute as if she couldn't remember why she was there and what to do next.

Ash's office—the crisp white brick, black shutters and bright red door—was right across the street. Despite every bit of craziness, these past few months had been some of the happiest she'd ever had and it was because of Ash and Levi. Ash had her heart, probably from the first time she saw him.

Jordan walked to the truck and sat in it, staring blindly out the window. She'd fought so hard not to feel anything for Ash, but every time she got to know him better a little piece of her heart and that wall she'd built around it crumbled.

She didn't want to live life without him but she also didn't want to make a decision for him that could— would—affect the rest of his life. Bertie had said that Jordan loved Levi enough to let him go if that was the best thing for him.

Did she love *Ash* enough that she would let him go if she thought it was the best thing for him? His childhood memories were still painful to him—memories of the hospital, of medical treatments and interventions. Would asking him to be a father to Levi be asking too much?

The idea of breaking things off with him felt like she was ripping her heart out with her bare hands, but… she did love him that much. She didn't want to tie him down to a life he didn't choose. And she was afraid, so afraid, that if she did, he would never forgive her.

* * *

Ash had a firm grip on Jordan's hand as they wound their way through the woods. He'd found her in the barn, hot and cranky, spitting mad at the goats, who had chewed a hole in the fence and gotten into the feed room in the barn. Luckily she found them before they ate enough to make them sick.

"Where are we going? Ash, I really don't have time to be wandering the forest—" she shot a look at him "—potentially lost for hours."

He laughed and pulled her deeper into the woods, where the trees were closer together. It was cooler here, the underbrush deep, but there was a trail and he knew where it led.

Jordan stopped talking and just followed his steps, her hand still gripped tightly in his.

"We used to play down here when I was a kid. I knew these woods better than I knew my own bedroom. My best friend Latham grew up on the property next to Red Hill Farm. If you haven't met him yet, you will." As he got deeper in the woods, his heart felt lighter, as if the years had been stripped away and he was a ten-year-old boy again, adventuring.

Jordan was quiet, much quieter than she normally was. She was stressed. He understood. All of the things that had been put on hold when Levi came to live with her pushed her further behind when they both got sick. The horse show with her clients was a big deal.

But this little side trip was stress relief. Ahead of them, he could see sunlight streaming through the trees and knew they were in the right place.

Thirty seconds later they broke through the tree line into a little pine straw-covered clearing. In the center was a small clear pool of water, about six feet across, but the best part about this little spot was the bubbling spring just above.

"What is this place?"

"It's a spring, like Red Hill Spring. This one is smaller and the yield is lower but it's private."

"It's beautiful."

The water was clear down to the rocks below. The bubbling of the creek sounded like music. He led Jordan to an overhang, slipped out of his loafers and sat.

She stood behind him, obviously reluctant.

"Sit down with me for a minute. Find your center and breathe a little and you'll be ready to go when you get back."

He'd never seen her so distracted. She took off her boots. One at a time they clunked onto the hard ground. When she rolled up her jeans, he knew he had her. Jordan dropped her feet into the water with a long, "Oh."

"Yeah, it's pretty great. Ice-cold, all year round, even in the middle of the summer. When I was a kid, Latham and I found some arrowheads not too far from here. Can you imagine Native Americans coming here to fill their jugs? We played like we were Native Americans for months."

She stared into the water. He didn't think she even heard him.

"What's going on, Jordan?"

"I talked to Reesa this morning. She said both parents signed the forms to relinquish their parental rights and if I want to adopt Levi, I need to let them know. Things will go fast now, like eight weeks, maybe."

He blinked, letting the words sink in. "So she was able to get the dad to sign, too."

"Apparently." Jordan looked into the clear, cold water. He wanted her to look at him.

"But that's amazing news!" He laughed, thinking about Levi being a part of their family for good, before he realized Jordan wasn't laughing, or smiling. "What's wrong?"

In response, she pulled her feet out of the water and rolled her socks back on, ignoring the fact that her feet were wet.

"Jordan?" She was scaring him.

She shoved her feet into her boots. "I thought a lot about whether I would be the best person to adopt Levi. I'm sure there are people out there more qualified to be a parent than I am, who could give him a better life. But the truth is, I'm the first mom he had who sat up with him through the night when he was scared, who gave him medicine when he was sick. I'm the one he's attached to. I'm the one he trusts."

"You're a great mom, Jordan. I see moms all the time and I would know." How could she not see how amazing she was with Levi?

"I can make the decision to parent Levi. I love him and whatever happens, I know I will still love him. I'm willing to take the risk on all the rest of it. But I can't make that decision for anyone else. That's just not fair. It's too much to ask."

She had him at such a disadvantage and he was achingly aware that while he had told her exactly how he felt about her, she hadn't returned the favor. He stood, and when he spoke, his voice was as cold as the spring water. "I don't think I know what you mean, Jordan."

"This—us—it was a stupid idea, anyway. Just look at us. I'm jeans and flannel. You're khaki and oxford cloth. I'm boots and trucks and you're loafers and a Lexus. I'm ball cap and braids and you wear bow ties. How mismatched can two people be?"

He stood there in his bare feet on the bank of the spring, his khakis rolled up around his ankles. "You're looking at this the wrong way, Jordan. You're looking with your eyes and your mind. You have to look with your heart."

"I'm looking at *you*. I'm not willing to take a gamble with your life. That's not my decision to make. And I'm scared, Ash." Her voice broke.

He slid his fingers down her arm, curving them around her wrist, taking a moment to really look at her. Her nostrils were flared, her pulse racing, full-out panic.

Ash took a step toward her, willing her to see how he felt. "You fight for love every day, Jordan. It's what you do. What you *live* for. You fight for Levi. Please… fight for us."

Her throat worked. She whispered, "I'm just not sure I can."

When she walked away this time, he let her go.

Somehow she'd convinced herself that she was doing this for him, that she was letting him go for his own good. She was overwhelmed right now, with work and responsibility, and she'd flat-out admitted she was scared.

The anger slowly drained out of him, just leaving sadness behind.

She'd had the idea at one time that he was a real ladies' man. Maybe he had been if that meant he went out with a lot of different people and didn't settle down. He thought that she'd gotten beyond that idea, but maybe she was afraid that if things got hard, he wouldn't stick, that he'd always be looking for the next best thing.

He loved Jordan, wanted her and Levi in his life, no matter what. But if she didn't believe it, where did he go from here? How could he show her that they were worth a fight?

Jordan put Levi to bed and went into the kitchen for a glass of iced tea. She was sad. And tired. And broken.

The front door cracked open. Claire stuck her head in and, once she got a look at Jordan's face, brought the rest of herself into the small cottage. She had a pint of rocky road and two spoons in her hand.

Jordan didn't smile. "I'm not really in the mood for ice cream."

"What? This is more serious than I thought. What's going on? I brought ice cream because you've been working so hard and you deserve a break." She set the ice cream on the island and turned toward Jordan. "What's wrong?"

"I found out that Levi is going to be free for adoption. They want me to adopt him."

Claire's eyes clouded with confusion. "Okay...?"

"And I broke up with Ash." Her breath hitched as she said it.

"Oh, Jordan. I'm so sorry. What happened?"

Jordan snapped the top off the ice cream and stabbed it with a spoon. "It's complicated."

"Complicated like he cheated and you wanted to kill him but you can't go to jail because you have a kid now, so instead you just broke up with him?" Claire brandished the spoon like a sword.

Jordan stared at her sister. "No. Where do you even come up with this stuff?"

Claire dug her spoon into the ice cream and took a bite. "If you would spill, I wouldn't have to use my imagination. Just tell me if I need to beat him up. I would do it."

"I know you would. I love that about you." The smile on Jordan's face was fleeting. "I made the decision to adopt Levi. But I can't make that decision for someone else. It's not fair. We don't know what level of care Levi is going to require."

"It's scary. I know it is. None of the kids we're raising have normal reactions to anything. I don't think Ash would be scared by this, though." Claire dug around in the ice cream for the chocolate-covered almonds.

"He wasn't upset. He was mad." Jordan put the spoon down. "He's got a right to be. I didn't handle it well."

"Did you ask him if he still wants to be in a relationship if you adopt Levi?"

"No. I didn't want to pressure him. That wouldn't prove anything."

"Maybe not, but I don't think a conversation would hu—" Her sister got a look at Jordan's face and stopped midsentence. "I'm sure you're right."

"I wouldn't trade being Levi's mom for anything. I love that little boy so much. He had no choice about who his parents were, or being abused, but I have the choice to stand for him from here on out."

"Yes, of course. But?" Her sister's hand automatically went to her belly.

"I'm in love with Ash." Jordan's eyes filled with tears and she closed her eyes and sniffed. "I didn't plan it. It just happened."

"Oh, Jordan." Claire's eyes went wide. "Did you tell him?"

"No. He said it to me, but I didn't—couldn't—say it back. I'm so stupid."

Claire wrapped her arms around Jordan's neck, like she used to when they were little. "A little bit. But we'll figure out something."

Jordan didn't know how they could possibly fix this. She was stuck between two things she wanted desperately and couldn't see any way to have one without giving up the other.

Chapter Seventeen

"Our first group of riders are the youngest equestrians at Triple H." Jordan's voice carried from the rented speakers to the crowd of parents and grandparents. Multicolored bunting hung from the eaves of the barn, fluttering in the wind. The horses—and the ring—were groomed to perfection.

She should be over the moon. This show was what she had dreamed of since she started her nonprofit. But instead of elation, she just felt exhausted.

Her finger kept her place in her notes as the volunteers led each rider in. There were three volunteers with each horse for the young set, one on each side to "catch" and one leading. Arabella, an adorable five-year-old girl with Down Syndrome, was up next.

"Arabella is five years old and her favorite food is cupcakes." The little girl's mom had dressed her in a cowgirl outfit with hot-pink boots, and as Arabella did her circle around the ring, she blew kisses to the crowd, who ate it up. "Arabella is riding Bartlet and she is being escorted by Lila, Cate and Violet."

Their spectators cheered as loudly for the volunteers as they did for their kids. More than a few of their dedicated volunteers had tears in their eyes as they left the ring.

"Our final rider in this group is Levi Wheeler." The kids from Red Hill Farm went crazy. Jordan tried to speak, but she was so proud of Levi and so overwhelmed that the words only squeaked out. "Levi is three years old and he's up on Leo today. His favorite food is—"

"Cookies!" Levi shouted from Leo's back, which drew a hoot of laughter and only added to the lump in Jordan's throat. When he first came to her, he didn't speak and had no confidence in himself or anyone else. Her little guy had come so far.

The volunteers stopped Leo in front of the parents. "Levi is being escorted by Amelia, Jonah and Everleigh."

As the five youngest riders took their last walk around the ring, Jordan searched the crowd for Ash. She had been sure that he would come for Levi, but he was nowhere in the crowd.

And that hurt, too.

There were two more groups of escorted riders. The final group was three teenagers. Two of those rode alone to circle the ring and one was escorted by Amelia on horseback. She had to hand it to this crowd. They were as enthusiastic for the last rider as they had been for the first.

When the last rider had left the ring, Jordan walked to the center. She was dressed in jeans and boots. No flannel in June in Alabama, but she had a T-shirt on with the Triple H logo on the pocket, like the volunteers wore when they came out.

"Before we go, I'd like to thank our volunteers. If you see someone wearing a bright orange shirt like this, please say thank you. Not one of them gets paid except in smiles and kisses. We couldn't operate Triple H without them, especially this one, my assistant, Allison."

Allison stepped into place beside Jordan. She wore a volunteer T-shirt, too, over white jeans that somehow didn't get dirty. She also had her hair done and a dozen thin gold bangles on her wrist. Jordan had no idea how she did it.

Jordan looked around. "I just have a few announcements before we adjourn for cookies and punch. Starting this month, we're taking reservations for a Royal Birthday or Cowpoke Party on Saturdays. I have some brochures for anyone interested. We'll also be offering a select few riding lessons in the slots we don't have clients. And finally, we'll be hosting a Fun Night on the Farm in October and part of the fun will be a silent auction. Please ask around and collect donations when you can.

"Finally, I'd like to thank you, the parents, for trusting us with your precious kids. We love them and are so grateful for the privilege to share them with you. Thank you so much for coming."

Allison took the mic from her with a sly smile. "Before we adjourn for cookies and punch, I want to add thanks to one other person without whom all this would not be possible. Triple H started with one person who had a dream and worked her heart out to make it happen. Thank you, Jordan."

Allison threw her arms around Jordan until she was gasping for air as the cheers and applause from the audience poured over her. She hadn't done this—any of this—for applause or thanks, but it was so nice to hear it and know that Triple H made a difference in people's lives.

She spent the next half hour taking pictures with the kids and the horses. It made her mad that this horse show was the culmination of so much hard work, and her mind was on Ash Sheehan.

"This was wonderful. The weather. The kids. The horses. It was absolutely perfect." Allison caught her arm and took a good look at her face. "Except that's not the face of someone who had an absolutely perfect morning. Are you okay?"

Jordan nodded. "Cover for me? I just need a few minutes."

Allison's eyes were full of questions, but she nodded. "No worries. I got this."

Jordan stepped through the fence into the ring and caught Leo's reins. She swung into the saddle and kicked her surprised horse into a trot.

She turned him into the woods and slowed to a walk. She needed to be on her horse and she needed to take a deep breath, maybe a few of them. The sun was high in the sky, but the woods were cool. Leo took advantage of her momentary inattention to munch on some honeysuckle.

"Come on, old buddy, stick with me here." The trail seemed much shorter on horseback. It wasn't long before she broke through the trees into the small clearing where she'd broken up with Ash.

She slid to the ground and let Leo have a drink of the clear, cold water. She closed her eyes and listened to the bubbling spring. For hundreds of years at least, people had been coming to this spring for water, for refreshment. They came tired and thirsty and they left renewed.

She wondered if any of them had been afraid they were making the wrong decision, settling here with their family, or moving their children to a strange land. Either way, they hadn't let their anxiety cripple them.

That was exactly what she had been doing, letting her fear take control of her decisions. She wasn't going to do that anymore. So she didn't know what was going to happen with Levi; no one could see the future for their kids.

And Ash—he had done everything possible to show her that he cared about her, and when it really mattered, she pushed him away. Worse, she had pointed out differences that didn't matter a whit. She didn't care what he wore or drove or what kind of shoes were on his feet. It was the man that she loved.

She *loved* him.

She loved him and she trusted him. Letting him go had been the biggest mistake of her life and she needed to tell him that. He may not take her back, but she had to put fear behind her and take a chance.

Ash sat at the island in the farmhouse kitchen, sulking. Joe was shoveling baby cereal into Sweetness's mouth at a frightening pace.

"I don't understand why you don't just go out there. If you want to see Levi ride, go see Levi ride. You're a grown man. Make the decision and do it."

Ash took a drink of his diet root beer and scowled. "I told her I was a relationship risk. I was honest. She should've told me..." The words trailed off. He didn't even care if he finished his thought. He was so done talking about it.

His brother was not. "Told you what?"

"That she didn't love me. Instead, she let me believe that she was falling in love with me, too." Ash pressed his fingers to his eyelids as if stopping the pain that seared through his head would stop the pain in his heart.

Joe tossed a handful of puffs onto the baby's tray. "Dude. I think you're missing something here. Also, you need to eat. You're getting a little maudlin. Maybe it's your blood sugar."

Snagging an apple from the bowl on the island, Joe put it on the cutting board and whacked it into pieces. He grabbed the warehouse club-sized jar of peanut butter and a serving spoon and shoved it all at Ash. "Eat this."

Ash dipped an apple slice into a spoon of peanut butter while his brother flipped around a bar stool and sat on it, his muscular forearms resting on the back, feet hooked on the rails.

"Ash, listen to me. Everyone is a relationship risk. But in this case, Jordan and Claire have good reason to be a little gun-shy. Their biological mother died when they were newborns and it was their biological father who gave them up for adoption."

He narrowed his eyes at his brother. "I didn't know that."

"Then their first adoptive family wanted them until Jordan had to have heart surgery and it was the dad who wanted to back out. They were raised by a single mother. It just isn't their experience that men have sticking power. In fact, it's the opposite."

"I didn't walk away from her. She did the walking."

"Maybe because she didn't want you to feel trapped. Or maybe she's scared that with Levi, it's just too much. It would be, for a lot of people."

"It's not for me. I love her and I love that little boy."

Joe shrugged. "You need to tell her that. Think of a way to show her. She's signing the adoption papers on Monday."

Sweetness squealed in the high chair.

Ash stood up. "I'll get her. I think I heard crying upstairs."

"There's always somebody crying in this house, but in this case, Josiah is the only one here. He was taking a nap and the other kids are with Claire watching the horse show." Joe started down the hall as Ash unlatched the high chair and picked up his foster niece. She promptly stuck her finger up his nose.

"That's not cute, Sweetness." Ash took her out the front, away from the hullabaloo of the horse show, patting her back and bouncing a little as she put her head on his shoulder. Full tummy, sleepy baby.

He paced the front porch, which suited Sweetness and calmed his ragged nerves. How did a guy who was a serial dater, a confirmed bachelor and a die-hard relationship-avoider get into this situation? He was—he almost gagged at the thought—lovesick over Jordan. He just had a talk about relationships with his brother.

There was only one explanation. He couldn't live without her. He didn't want to live without her. And somehow, he had to show her that he was in this for the long haul. He was sticking.

Right then the thought struck him that maybe he hadn't been fully committed to Jordan. He'd shared some things with her but he hadn't shared his deepest fears and his wildest hopes.

In so many ways, their fears were the same—that their brokenness would be too big for the other person to handle. But they were in it together. She didn't just hold his heart in her hands, he held hers, as well.

As he cradled the now-sleeping foster baby, whom he had chosen to love as a part of his family, he understood that he was at a crossroads in so many ways. His life was about more than just being a good person and doing good things. He needed to be fully committed, no holding back.

He pushed open the door to the big, old farmhouse and placed Sweetness in her crib. He had some planning to do.

Sunday afternoon Jordan folded the bunting into a Rubbermaid tub with the rest of the supplies for their horse show. These would go into the attic of the barn until the next time they were needed, probably sometime next fall.

Mrs. Matthews was putting Levi to bed and Jordan was going to find Ash. She'd swapped her jeans for khaki shorts and her boots for wedge heels and a pinpoint oxford cloth shirt that she tied at the waist.

It was hard to admit, even to herself, how wrong she had been. Jeans and flannel were comfortable, but she could step out of her comfort zone for someone as important to her as Ash.

The horses had been let out to pasture, tack cleaned and put away. One of the cats wound through her legs, her belly fat with babies again. Jordan had no more excuses to procrastinate. She was closing the tack room door when she heard the sound of a huge engine idling outside the barn.

She slipped the padlock into the latch and clicked it closed before walking through the open door. A huge red truck sat in the driveway, so shiny she could see her face in the mint new paint job. The driver's-side door opened and one booted foot stepped onto the running board.

Like the truck, the boots were shiny new leather and she thought, *Greenhorn.*

And then the fingers curved around the door and her heart rate picked up. She knew those fingers.

Ash slammed the door and walked toward her, swaggering a little. She caught her bottom lip between her teeth, hiding a smile.

With the brand-new boots, he had on jeans that were snug in the seat and just a little worn. She swallowed hard. He had on a *Stand Up to Cancer* T-shirt with a flannel plaid shirt loose over it, sleeves rolled up.

She shook her head, not sure whether to laugh or cry. "What are you doing?"

He took a few steps toward her and winced. She imagined the brand-new boots were pinching, and her heart felt like it might explode.

A couple more steps put him square in front of her. He reached for her hands and she slid them into his. She looked at their joined hands. Her voice was soft. "I'm sorry I walked away from you the other day at the spring. I was wrong."

He shook his head.

She smiled. "No, I was wrong. We're not mismatched. We're boots and loafers and flannel and ox-ford cloth and khaki and denim and we complement each other perfectly. I love you, Ash, and my life isn't the same without you in it."

Ash gave her fingers a tug and somehow she ended up in his arms. "You have no idea how much I wanted to hear you say that. Can you go for a ride with me in my new truck?"

"Yes. Mrs. Matthews is putting Levi to bed."

He drove them to the river house, pulling to a stop and jumping down first, so he could open the door for her. "I want to show you something."

Her stomach was in knots, but she nodded and slid her hand into his. They walked around to the front of the house that looked over the river. The sun was going down, a huge red ball in the sky, when she saw it. He had built a ramp leading from the driveway to his front porch. Her eyes welled. "Ash."

He turned her toward him—this amazing, generous soul—and she looked into his beautiful Sheehan-blue eyes. "When I walk around my house and imagine what it will look like finished, I see you. I see Levi playing in the front yard and fishing off the dock with me. I don't just want a relationship with you, Jordan, I want a future, our future. I love every boot-loving, jeans-wearing, flannel-clad inch of you."

Jordan laughed, but her chest so tight with emotion, she could barely breathe. "I come with strings attached. Are you really sure you're okay with that?"

"I come with strings, too. It's choosing to love each other that matters. I choose you. And I choose Levi. Every day, from now on."

Ash pulled the ring out of his pocket, an opal surrounded with deep red rubies. "Please marry me, Jordan."

She held out her left hand, fingers trembling, and he slid the ring onto her finger. "Perfect fit."

Epilogue

"One small thing," Ash said as they pulled into the farm. There was already a line of cars parked halfway out to the highway. "I'd really like to get married tonight. When you sign the adoption paperwork saying you want to be Levi's mom, I want to be there promising to be his dad."

"I love the idea, but I'm signing the adoption agreement paperwork tomorrow." She looked out the window. "What are all these cars doing here?"

His heart was hammering inside his chest as he parked the truck next to the farmhouse. Why had he thought this was a good idea? "If you're okay with it, we're having a wedding tonight. If you're not okay with it, we'll have a big party and pretend this never happened."

"What are you talking about? We can't get married tonight!" Her voice was a high squeak. "I'm wearing shorts! There's no plan!"

There was a knock on the passenger-side window of Ash's brand-new truck. Claire pulled the door open. She, Wynn and Allison stood in a semicircle around the open door. Their dresses were different styles, each a shade of pale blue.

Claire's eyes were suspiciously shiny, but she held out a hand to Jordan. "We're your bridal party. We have everything you need inside. Come on. We have a lot to do!"

Jordan looked back at Ash. Her eyes were wide and sending him a message. Something like, *I love you and can't wait to marry you.* Or it could be, *I'm gonna kill you when all these people are gone.* He wasn't quite sure which.

She reached back into the truck and grabbed his hand. "Are you sure you want to do this?"

"I've never been more sure of anything in my life. I love you, Jordan."

She nodded. "Okay. Okay. We're really doing this."

He got out of the truck and watched as the women led her into the house to get ready. He was getting married tonight!

The guys had the lights strung across the backyard and the twins were setting up chairs. His mother bustled by with a big box of flowers, stopping to give him a one-armed hug. "I could just kill you for doing this on such short notice, but I'm so ridiculously proud of you."

"Thanks, Mom. I love her. Now, does anyone know where my son is?"

Joe looked over from where he was stretching an extension cord across the yard to where the band was setting up. "Yeah, he's at the cottage with Mrs. Matthews. Your clothes and the ones Claire got for him are in his room."

Ash walked around the pond to the small cottage where Jordan lived with Levi. He found Mrs. Matthews sitting on the floor with Levi and his blocks. Ash smiled at Levi and would have sworn he could feel his heart expanding. "Hey, Mrs. Matthews. I've got him from here."

Levi looked up with a big toothy grin. "Doc!"

Mrs. Matthews stood and gathered her book and reading glasses. "I don't mind staying."

"Thank you very much, but me and the little guy here need to have a man-to-man talk."

She patted his hand as she passed him. "All right, then. I'll see you boys in a few minutes."

Ash lifted Levi into his arms and walked to the window, where they could see the preparations taking place in the backyard. "You see those pretty lights over there? We're having a big party because your mama is getting married."

Levi pointed. "Mama?"

"Yes, buddy, Mama is right over there getting ready. And we're going to get ready, too, because today is a big day. We're going to be a family."

Levi pointed out the window again. "Mama?"

"That's right. You and me and Mama. I'm gonna be your dad." His eyes were stinging with tears.

Levi turned big brown eyes on Ash. "Dad?"

"That's right." Ash forced the words over the huge lump in his throat. A tear tracked down his cheek when those little arms latched around his neck. "I'm the luckiest dad in the whole world. Now we better get ready, because Aunt Claire will not be happy if we're late."

Jordan stood at the kitchen door—dressed in a tea-length lace gown and cowboy boots—and watched her best friends walk down the aisle between the chairs on the back lawn. Allison had piled Jordan's hair on top of her head and Wynn had done her makeup. She'd held their hands as they prayed for her and Ash and their new life, just beginning to unfold.

Someone had taken the swing down and decorated the arch with flowers and twinkle lights. In less than five minutes, she would walk out that door and down the steps and promise that she would love Ash forever. It was fitting that they would get married under the big old oak tree. She prayed that their roots as a couple would grow deep, their arms would stretch wide and their love would cast shade for those who needed it.

With tears in her eyes, Claire handed Jordan a bouquet of hydrangeas and lilies that Bertie had picked in her backyard. She caught her twin in a hug. "I wish Mom was here to see how beautiful you are. I love you."

"I love you, too."

"Okay, here I go, before I cry all my mascara off." Claire walked slowly down the wide steps of the old house and down the aisle, and then it was Jordan's turn.

Joe offered his arm as Jordan stepped over the threshold. He would walk her down the aisle to give her away.

It was a beautiful night, stars scattered in the vast sky, and below, all the people she loved, gathered to witness the start of a new family.

When she started down the aisle, she saw Ash waiting for her at the altar, Levi held safe in his strong arms. Joy exploded in her chest. They were hers, these two men, beyond all reason and logic.

She realized, finally, that she didn't have to listen to that voice, the one telling her she didn't deserve this family, this life. Maybe she and Ash weren't perfect, but they had each other and they weren't giving up.

And that was the lesson, she thought, as she stepped into place beside Ash. You didn't give up. You never gave up. You kept trying and trying until the trying became the joy.

It was the journey that was beautiful, not how it ended.

And she and Ash had a beautiful journey ahead.

* * * * *

*If you loved this story,
pick up the other book
in the* FAMILY BLESSINGS *series,*

THE DAD NEXT DOOR

from author Stephanie Dees.

*Available now from Love Inspired!
Find more great reads at www.LoveInspired.com*

Dear Reader,

I love a good calendar! It's always a big decision which planner I'll use for the next year. I replenish my supplies—pens, sticky notes, stickers—and I delight in filling in the little squares with my lists and checking off my daily tasks.

In *A Baby for the Doctor*, Jordan has plans. She's busy starting a business. She isn't prepared for a child in her life and she definitely doesn't have time for romance! She's surprised when God leads her to both and struggles to understand His plans for her.

Sometimes I'm like that, too, and I struggle with laying aside my tasks to follow God's plan. It takes faith to put down the to-do list and step out into the unknown, but it's when we put aside our agenda and follow God's that we find true joy and fulfillment.

Thanks for joining me again in Red Hill Springs! I'd love to hear from you! Find me at my website www.stephaniedees.com or on Facebook!

Wishing you all the best,
Steph

Get 2 Free Books,
Plus 2 Free Gifts—
just for trying the Reader Service!

YES! Please send me 2 FREE Love Inspired® Romance novels and my 2 FREE mystery gifts (gifts are worth about $10 retail). After receiving them, if I don't wish to receive any more books, I can return the shipping statement marked "cancel." If I don't cancel, I will receive 6 brand-new novels every month and be billed just $5.24 for the regular-print edition or $5.74 each for the larger-print edition in the U.S., or $5.74 each for the regular-print edition or $6.24 each for the larger-print edition in Canada. That's a saving of at least 13% off the cover price. It's quite a bargain! Shipping and handling is just 50¢ per book in the U.S. and 75¢ per book in Canada.* I understand that accepting the 2 free books and gifts places me under no obligation to buy anything. I can always return a shipment and cancel at any time. The free books and gifts are mine to keep no matter what I decide.

Please check one:

☐ Love Inspired Romance Regular-Print
(105/305 IDN GLWW)

☐ Love Inspired Romance Larger-Print
(122/322 IDN GLWW)

Name _____ (PLEASE PRINT) _____

Address _____ Apt. # _____

City _____ State/Province _____ Zip/Postal Code _____

Signature (if under 18, a parent or guardian must sign)

Mail to the **Reader Service:**
IN U.S.A.: P.O. Box 1341, Buffalo, NY 14240-8531
IN CANADA: P.O. Box 603, Fort Erie, Ontario L2A 5X3

Want to try two free books from another line?
Call 1-800-873-8635 today or visit www.ReaderService.com.

*Terms and prices subject to change without notice. Prices do not include applicable taxes. Sales tax applicable in N.Y. Canadian residents will be charged applicable taxes. Offer not valid in Quebec. This offer is limited to one order per household. Books received may not be as shown. Not valid for current subscribers to Love Inspired Romance books. All orders subject to approval. Credit or debit balances in a customer's account(s) may be offset by any other outstanding balance owed by or to the customer. Please allow 4 to 6 weeks for delivery. Offer available while quantities last.

Your Privacy—The Reader Service is committed to protecting your privacy. Our Privacy Policy is available online at www.ReaderService.com or upon request from the Reader Service.

We make a portion of our mailing list available to reputable third parties that offer products we believe may interest you. If you prefer that we not exchange your name with third parties, or if you wish to clarify or modify your communication preferences, please visit us at www.ReaderService.com/consumerschoice or write to us at Reader Service Preference Service, P.O. Box 9062, Buffalo, NY 14240-9062. Include your complete name and address.

LI17R2

SPECIAL EXCERPT FROM

Love Inspired®

When Erica Lindholm and her twin babies show up at his family farm just before Christmas, Jason Stephanidis can tell she's hiding something. But how can he refuse the young mother, a friend of his sister's, a place to stay during the holidays? He never counted on wanting Erica and the boys to be a more permanent part of his life...

Read on for a sneak peek of
SECRET CHRISTMAS TWINS
by **Lee Tobin McClain**,
part of the **CHRISTMAS TWINS** miniseries.

Once both twins were bundled, snug between Papa and Erica, Jason sent the horses trotting forward. The sun was up now, making millions of diamonds on the snow that stretched across the hills far into the distance. He smelled pine, a sharp, resin-laden sweetness.

When he picked up the pace, the sleigh bells jingled.

"Real sleigh bells!" Erica said, and then, as they approached the white covered bridge decorated with a simple wreath for Christmas, she gasped. "This is the most beautiful place I've ever seen."

Jason glanced back, unable to resist watching her fall in love with his home.

Papa was smiling for the first time since he'd learned of Kimmie's death. And as they crossed the bridge and trotted toward the church, converging with other horse-drawn sleighs, Jason felt a sense of rightness.

Mikey started babbling to Teddy, accompanied by gestures and much repetition of his new word. Teddy tilted his head to one side and burst forth with his own stream of nonsense syllables, seeming to ask a question, batting Mikey on the arm. Mikey waved toward the horses and jabbered some more, as if he were explaining something important.

They were such personalities, even as little as they were. Jason couldn't help smiling as he watched them interact.

Once Papa had the reins set and the horses tied up, Jason jumped out of the sleigh, and then turned to help Erica down. She handed him a twin. "Can you hold Mikey?"

He caught a whiff of baby powder and pulled the little one tight against his shoulder. Then he reached out to help Erica, and she took his hand to climb down, Teddy on her hip.

When he held her hand, something electric seemed to travel right to his heart. Involuntarily he squeezed and held on.

She drew in a sharp breath as she looked at him, some mixture of puzzlement and awareness in her eyes.

What was Erica's secret?

And wasn't it curious that, after all these years, there were twins in the farmhouse again?

Don't miss
SECRET CHRISTMAS TWINS
by Lee Tobin McClain, available November 2017
wherever Love Inspired® books and ebooks are sold.

www.LoveInspired.com

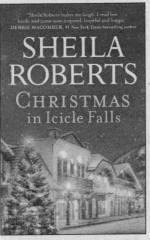

Love Inspired®

Inspirational Romance to Warm Your Heart and Soul

Join our social communities to connect with other readers who share your love!

Sign up for the Love Inspired newsletter at **www.LoveInspired.com** to be the first to find out about upcoming titles, special promotions and exclusive content.

CONNECT WITH US AT:

Harlequin.com/Community

 Facebook.com/LoveInspiredBooks

Twitter.com/LoveInspiredBks

LISOCIAL2017